APR 2 2 2015

D0933383

# The Pot Thief
# Who Studied
# Billy the Kid

FEB 2 8 2019

# The Pot Thief Who Studied Billy the Kid

*A Pot Thief Mystery*

## J. MICHAEL ORENDUFF

OPEN ROAD ROAD
INTEGRATED MEDIA
NEW YORK

WILLARD LIBRARY, BATTLE CREEK, MI

All rights reserved, including without limitation the right to reproduce this book or any portion thereof in any form or by any means, whether electronic or mechanical, now known or hereinafter invented, without the express written permission of the publisher.

This is a work of fiction. Names, characters, places, events, and incidents either are the product of the author's imagination or are used fictitiously. Any resemblance to actual persons, living or dead, businesses, companies, events, or locales is entirely coincidental.

Copyright © 2013 by J. Michael Orenduff

Cover design by Kathleen Lynch

ISBN 978-1-4804-5862-8

This edition published in 2014 by Open Road Integrated Media, Inc.
345 Hudson Street
New York, NY 10014
www.openroadmedia.com

*To my sister Pat*
*who explored the Lincoln County Courthouse*
*and other haunts of Billy the Kid with me when we were kids.*
*And to Richard, my brother-in-law and friend.*

# The Pot Thief Who Studied Billy the Kid

"I would rather write another book than be rich." —Lew Wallace

"Amen." —J. Michael Orenduff

# 1

I was on a ledge three hundred feet above the Rio Doloroso violating two federal laws, one on purpose and the other by accident.

I felt like Indiana Jones. Except I was afraid to approach the precipice. But my acrophobia didn't stop me from digging. I'd been told there were ancient pots here, and I knew they would be back in the ruins, not out on the rim.

I'm not a professional archaeologist and I didn't have a permit to excavate, so the first law I was breaking was the Archaeological Resources Protection Act (ARPA).

So what?

Because of the American Bar Association, it would be impossible today for Abe Lincoln to be a lawyer.

Because of the Institute of Electrical and Electronics Engineers, it would be impossible today for Thomas Edison to be an electrical engineer.

And thanks to the Archaeological Institute of America, it's also impossible for me to hunt for artifacts legally. Which was why I was digging under cover of darkness.

Every association of 'professionals' wants to exclude amateurs. So Congress caved in to the wishes of professional archaeologists back in the eighties and passed ARPA.

My name is Hubert Schuze, and I'm a treasure hunter. Congress redefined me as a pot thief, but it also passed a health care program with a price tag of 940 billion dollars and called it the 'Affordable Health Care Act'. They aren't exactly experts when it comes to truth in labeling.

Here's a message for my representatives in Washington—Health care is not affordable and most archaeological resources do not need protecting.

If they're resources, we should exploit them. That's what I do, and I'm positive that's what the people who created them would want.

I'm a potter myself. After I'm long dead, I don't want the pots I made mouldering in the ground like John Brown's body. I want some enterprising lad like myself to dig them up, appreciate them and make a few bucks in the process. Maybe he can earn enough to see a doctor.

I do feel bad about the second law I was breaking, the Native American Graves Protection and Repatriation Act (NAGPRA). Who other than a ghoul would violate that one?

But it wasn't my fault. I was digging in a ruin of residences. Prehistoric tribes didn't bury their dead in their living quarters. So you can imagine my surprise when I stuck my hand into the hole I'd dug and grasped another hand.

I'd been hoping for an artifact, not a handshake.

It gets worse.

One of the tools I use is a piece of rebar. Knowing this would make professional archaeologists bite the bristles off their little bitty brushes. But the success rate is low in treasure hunting. I can't afford to waste time digging in dry holes. So I use the rebar to probe through soft soil and discover whether there is anything solid below the surface.

When I feel the slightest resistance, I set the rebar aside and dig with my hands. I don't want to damage any potential merchandise. Usually what I find is a rock or a root.

The rebar had bumped a pot shard in the first area I dug. It wasn't big enough to be marketable. But it had an unusual design I'd never seen and a long graceful curve I wanted to see if I could duplicate. I pocketed it.

As I was about to start a second hole, some sand pelted me from the overhang above. I yelled up to Geronimo to stay away from the edge, but he never listens to me. And it could just as easily have been a crow or a chipmunk.

Too bad I didn't move after the sand hit me. For it was in the second location that my rebar's advance through the soil was impeded by the aforementioned hand. I had accidentally desecrated human remains.

I felt woozy. The *chorizo* I'd wolfed down for energy gurgled up my esophagus. I swallowed hard to keep it down.

Then I heard an even louder gurgling.

It wasn't my tummy rumbling. It was the sound of my Bronco's clutch being engaged. Most people don't know what a clutch sounds like. They have shiny new cars with automatic transmissions. Drop it in drive and go. But my thirty-two-year-old clutch doesn't grab like it used to. Like its forty-something-year-old owner, it slips and grinds before it moves forward.

I had left Geronimo with the Bronco. And while he sometimes displays a certain canine cunning, I didn't think he was capable of starting the thing. But couldn't he at least have barked at the car thief?

It wasn't that I minded much about losing the vehicle. But the rope that had lowered me down to the ruin—and by means of which I planned to ascend back to the surface—was attached to the winch.

I was stranded in a prehistoric cliff dwelling three hundred feet above the river below and thirty feet below the ground above.

Thirty feet is not that far. If it isn't too steep, you could just walk up it. But then your enemies could come down it just as easily, which would defeat the purpose of a cliff dwelling.

Even if it were a perfectly vertical cliff, you could perhaps work your way up using little rock fissures as hand and toe holds. But when the cliff is *past* vertical, when it slants away from the direction you want to go, the only way up is by rope.

Like the one I had just watched disappear.

Of course there was another way out. There would be a path cut into the cliff that would take me to a point where the terrain allowed a narrow switchback climb up to the surface. Ancient cliff dwellers sought places with an overhang for protection and a narrow entrance path that could be easily guarded. One man can hold off an entire raiding party if they have to approach single file. He just stands behind a big rock next to the narrowest part of the path and pushes them over the edge as they creep along.

Just the thought of that narrowest part of the path made me break out in a cold sweat.

# 2

Unless I wanted to spend the rest of my life in a cliff dwelling, I had to find that path and follow it.

But I wasn't going to risk it at night. And I wasn't going to sleep next to a partially open grave. So I filled the hole and gently packed down the soil. I don't know any prayers for reinterment, but I said what came to mind and meant every word of it.

I had my first aid kit, water, matches, a flashlight and a warm jacket with a pocket full of *chorizo*. It wasn't everything you'd take on a wilderness camping trip, but it was enough.

I also had a large gunny sack. I didn't get to carry a pot or two home in it as I had hoped, but it did come in handy in several ways. My final piece of equipment was the rebar, one end of which had recently poked a human hand.

I thought about tossing it over the ledge into the Rio Doloroso. But the way my luck was running, it would probably impale some wilderness trekker asleep in his tent. I didn't need that on my conscience, so I just stuck the thing in the ground, evil end first.

I rolled the jacket up for a pillow and bedded down behind what remained of a rock and mud wall. Maybe the prayer had cleansed my mind because I dropped off to sleep almost immediately.

The first time I woke up, it was because of the cold. I put the jacket on. The gunny sack was not substantial enough to make much of a pillow, but at least it saved me from having to sleep with my head directly on the ground.

The second time I woke up, it was because of the rustling sound.

There was no wind. Something was moving through the brush. And getting nearer. I pulled the rebar out of the ground. Let it be a skunk, I thought, although it was making way too much noise to be one.

A skunk would be okay. Even a bobcat. They seldom attack humans. Just not a mountain lion. Or worse, a badger. A badger would probably bite through the rebar before bulldozing me off the cliff.

It was just a few feet away. I could hear it panting. I raised the rebar above my head just as it broke into the clearing and leapt at me.

It would've served him right if I'd brained him with the piece of iron. He didn't bark to scare away the car thief, and he didn't bark to let me know he was approaching.

He's probably a mix of Irish setter and border collie. I suspect he's also part anteater. I don't think they bark. It would also explain the long neck that sags down and sways to and fro as he walks.

Despite the start he gave me, I was glad to see him. His feathery wagging tail and big sad eyes were part of it. But the main reason was that Geronimo's arrival confirmed the path was still there and passable. He may be part anteater, but he is certainly not part mountain goat. If he could make it down the path, I could make it back up.

He inhaled the *chorizo* I gave him then started digging at the soft dirt I had tamped down. My explanation about the Native American Graves Protection and Repatriation Act fell on deaf ears. See what I mean about him never listening to me?

So I put a heavy rock on top of the grave.

I guess I've seen too many old westerns because the sight of the rock put me in mind to construct a crude cross from two limbs and push it into the soft ground behind the rock. Then it occurred to me that someone born here five hundred years before Columbus was unlikely to have been a Christian.

I fell asleep thinking about what object or symbol might be appropriate for the grave.

And awoke for the third time to the sound of another critter coming down the trail. I have only one dog, so the same thoughts as before ran through my head except for the bear my overwrought imagination added to the mountain lion and the badger.

It was noisy and moving slowly.

And dragging a chain.

A chain?

On a cliff over the Rio Doloroso in the middle of nowhere?

I tried to imagine what it could be. The ghost of grave robbers past? The angry spirit of the corpse I had impaled?

Geronimo whined and scooted back against the cliff. I joined him. For all I know, I was also whining. I was giving serious consideration to taking a running leap into the Rio Doloroso if a bear or mountain lion appeared.

I figured there were two possibilities. The river would be dry, as it frequently is in late summer, and I would go splat on its rocky bed. Or I might land in water deep enough to survive the fall. Since I can't swim, I would drown. Both options seemed preferable to being eaten alive by a bear or mountain lion.

And what more appropriate place to die than one named *doloroso*?

But it was neither a bear nor a mountain lion. It was a young coyote dragging a chain attached to a trap clamped on his left front foot. I suppose he was young enough that his bones were still supple. The trap had not broken his leg. But it had done major damage. There was a lot of blood on his leg and quite a bit on his muzzle.

Stories of coyotes chewing off a foot to escape a trap are pure myth. He had blood on his muzzle because he had licked the wound, not because he had attempted self-amputation. How he managed to pull the stake out of the ground I don't know. Maybe the idiot who set the trap didn't anchor it properly.

I tossed a *chorizo* to him. He sniffed at it. He looked up at me with what looked to be a quizzical expression. Then he ate the *chorizo*.

He looked down at his leg then up at me. It's tempting to say he wanted help, but I don't believe coyotes see humans as helpers. The Wildlife Service kills over six thousand coyotes in New Mexico every year by trapping, snaring, shooting, poisoning and aerial gunning.

Yes, aerial gunning. They shoot them from helicopters and small planes. Keep that in mind the next time you see one of those highway signs that read, "speeding enforced by aircraft."

One moment you're motoring down the interstate. The next you're taken out by an air-to-surface missile.

# 3

Susannah said, "You look like death—"

"I know, 'warmed over'."

She shook her head. "No. You look like death *before* it was warmed over. While it was still cold and clammy."

The margarita in my hand was the best thing I'd ever tasted. Funny how a near-death experience makes you savor even the smallest pleasures.

"I don't care how I look. I feel terrific."

Susannah and I meet at *Dos Hermanas Tortilleria* almost every weekday at five for margaritas. I own a shop in Albuquerque's Old Town where I sell traditional Native American pottery and my own copies of ancient designs. As you already know, I get some of my merchandise by illegal excavation.

My days in the shop or at my potter's wheel are usually so boring that I mostly listen while Susannah talks. She has interesting things to report from her work as a waitress at *La Placita*, her night courses at the University of New Mexico and her star-crossed love life.

But on this cool August evening, I was recounting my harrowing night on the ledge and the even more harrowing experience that followed.

"You went down a rope hand over hand like a gymnast? That doesn't sound like something you could do."

"I don't know if I could do it because it's not something I would even try. I did use a rope, but all I had to do was hang on while the winch lowered me down."

"What was her name?"

"It wasn't that kind of a winch. It's the wind-up—"

"That was a joke, Hubie. I know what a winch is. I grew up on a ranch, remember? But how could you operate the winch while you were hanging on to a rope?"

"Just push the button on the remote control."

"Tristan?"

I nodded. Tristan is my nephew and a whiz with all things digital and technical. He's a full-time computer science major at the university and close to gaining a degree.

Susannah is in her late twenties and in no danger of graduating because she's part-time and has changed majors so often. It's art history at the moment.

I told her almost everything that happened that night including finding a hand where I was hoping for a pot. I left out the part about accidentally poking it with the rebar.

She shuddered. "That's awful. Has it ever happened to you before?"

I shook my head. "I dig in ruins and around places where the ancient ones might have gone for water. They wouldn't bury their dead in their houses or their watering holes, so I've never found human remains before and never expect to again."

"Then how do you explain finding a grave in a ruin?"

"It wasn't a grave. Like I said, no one buries their dead in their house."

"John Gacy buried twenty six people in the crawlspace of his."

Now it was my turn to shudder. "There were no serial killers among the Anasazi."

"So how do you explain it?"

I shrugged. "The only theory I've come up with is that the person died around the time the place was being abandoned. We know they relocated periodically, but we're not sure why. Maybe they needed more space, or their water supply dried up or a *tsiwi* advised them to move. Maybe the person I found went back to get something and died of a heart attack."

"*Tsiwi?*"

"It's one of many words for medicine men. It means 'those of the sweeping eyes'. But I suspect the people of that cliff dwelling wouldn't know that word. Their language probably died with them."

Her face lit up. "Maybe he wasn't one of them. Maybe he was a treasure hunter like you and died while searching for the same pots you were searching for."

Susannah has a vivid imagination and loves mysteries.

"No way. He was two feet under the ground. If he was a modern human who wandered into the ruin and died, he would be right on the surface."

"Why wouldn't one of the original cliff dwellers also be right on the surface if he died of natural causes?"

"Because a lot of dirt and debris can be deposited in a thousand years. This guy was far enough under that he had to be an original inhabitant."

She had a skeptical look. "How can you be sure?"

"I was in the graduate program in archaeology at UNM."

"Yeah, but they kicked you out before you got a degree."

"That's their problem."

She was right. I made my first significant find back in the eighties as a student on a summer dig. I knew the faculty leaders were digging in the wrong place as soon as I saw them drive the stakes and stretch the string.

They were jealous when I unearthed three rare pots from a spot I selected on my own. Even though treasure hunting was legal back then, they expelled me because I refused to give them the pots. I sold them instead and used the money to make a down payment on the building where I have my shop. I even had enough left over to buy the Bronco, but I guessed that part of the investment was now history.

After I told her about the coyote, she said, "Wait. A coyote actually let you remove a trap from his leg?"

"I'm not sure 'let' is the right word. He did let me get close to him. He'd lost a lot of blood and was probably weak and disoriented. And maybe he appreciated the *chorizo* I gave him. I made soothing noises as I approached."

She was giving me another skeptical look. "What sort of soothing noises?"

"Nice doggy, nice doggy."

"Coyotes are not dogs, Hubert."

"I know that. But 'nice coyote, nice coyote' didn't spring to mind, so I just went with what did. When I was near enough, I shoved a gunny sack over his head and pulled it taut. Then I jabbed the rebar between the teeth of the trap and pried it open. He yelped and squirmed in the sack, but when I took it off, he didn't bolt. I wish I hadn't had to use the gunny sack, but I didn't want to get bitten."

"And what was Geronimo doing while you were playing coyote whisperer?"

"He was raising his head towards the moon and pursing his lips. But no sound was forthcoming."

"Face it, Hubie. Your dog is weird,"

"That's because he's half anteater."

She rolled her eyes. "Right. So then what?"

"I gave each of us a ration of *chorizo* and we went to sleep."

"And how did you get back to civilization?"

"After we had breakfast—"

"More *chorizo*?"

"Right. I explained that Geronimo would lead the way since he knew the path, I would follow and Wiley would bring up the rear."

"Wiley?"

"Yeah. You know, Wile E. Coyote. Like in the Roadrunner cartoons."

"You named the coyote?"

"Why not? He looked a lot more like a dog than Geronimo."

"Sheesh. So then what?"

"I shoved Geronimo down the path and took a step after him. I looked back and told Wiley to follow, but when he put weight on his injured foot, he flopped back down. I went back and sat down a few feet away from him. He didn't seem to mind. So I opened the first aid kit and sprayed the wounded area with Bactine."

"So after you played vet, you went down the path?"

"No. I figured he needed time to let the anesthetic work. I gathered some wood and started a fire."

"And the three of you sat around the campfire singing *Kumbaya*."

I ignored her sarcasm. "Nope. Wiley fell asleep, Geronimo didn't know the words and I didn't feel like doing a solo. So I just sat there trying not to think about the path. As it turns out, that was the easiest part of the day."

# 4

The earnest young man entered my shop on July 14th. I remember the exact date because I'd finally finished reading *The Wooing of Malkatoon* by Lew Wallace and was calculating how long it had taken.

Four months to the day.

I'm not a slow reader. I just couldn't take more than a page or two a day. I probably completed sixty books during those four months, doing a few pages of *Malkatoon* in the lull between other books.

I stuck with it only because the centennial of New Mexico's statehood was coming up, and I'd decided to focus my reading on my native state. I selected Wallace because he was New Mexico's Territorial Governor from 1878 to 1881 during which time he published his most famous work, *Ben-Hur*. I was fascinated that someone who governed New Mexico during its Wild West days was also writing the book that eventually became the blockbuster movie starring Charlton Heston.

But all I was thinking about when the handsome young man passed over my threshold was how happy I was to be finished with *Malkatoon*. I felt like I deserved something for my persistence, and he delivered it, placing a small Anasazi bowl on my counter.

Or, more accurately, two pieces of a small Anasazi bowl. Joining them at their edges produced about two thirds of the original. Among serious collectors, anything over half is a bowl. Anything less is a shard.

I looked up at his honest face. "You want to sell this?"

"Make me an offer," he said.

I shook my head. "It doesn't work that way. Sellers set the price. If I like your price, I'll take it. If not, we can haggle. But you've got to start."

"You have me at a disadvantage. You're in the business. You know how much the pot is worth."

"Where did you get it?"

He hesitated. He looked to be around thirty. In addition to his honest face, he had a pleasant smile, intelligent eyes and a strong chin. "I got it from a teenager who knows about an ancient cliff dwelling near our village."

"Where?"

"At my office."

"I meant where is the cliff dwelling, not where did you get the pot."

"Let's talk price," he said.

I decided to ask about the location of the cliff dwelling later.

He glanced around the shop. "You have anything like this?"

I led him to a shelf on the west wall and pointed to an ancient pot. "This one is about the same size but in better shape. You can see I have it priced at three thousand."

"I'll take two for mine," he said.

"I'll give you five hundred."

"How about this?" he offered. "You give me a thousand for the pot, and I'll tell you where the cliff dwelling is."

"That won't do me any good if it's on a reservation. I don't hunt for artifacts on Indian lands."

"It's not on a reservation. It's on Bureau of Land Management land. But it's so remote and well-hidden that I don't think even they know it's there."

He had just described my ideal pot-digging location. "What's your name and where do you live?"

"Alvar Nuñez," he said. He'd been speaking perfect unaccented English, but his name rolled off his tongue as if we were in Jerez. "I live in a place you've never heard of."

"Try me."

"La Reina."

"Near the Taos County line with a great view of Cerro Roto?"

"You've been there? We're not even on state maps."

"I haven't been there. But my work requires study of the USGS topographic maps, so I've seen every place name in the state no matter how small."

I had him wait while I went to my residence in the back of the building and withdrew $1,000 from my secret hiding place. I also brought my topo maps back to the shop. He found the right map and marked the location of the ruin about twenty miles from the village.

Before I handed him the money, I asked to see his driver's license. It said Alvar Nuñez. And in a break with tradition, the picture on the license actually looked like him.

After I handed him the money, he counted it. On the trust scale, we were even.

And that's how I ended up a few weeks later stranded on the cliff dwelling above the Rio Doloroso.

# 5

I raised two fingers to signal our favorite server, Angie, that Susannah and I both needed refills.

"So what happened after the coyote woke up?" Susannah asked.

"Why don't you call him Wiley?"

"We don't give names to coyotes on our ranch."

"Do you shoot them from aircraft?"

"No. And we don't set traps or poison. The only time we ever shoot a coyote is when one approaches our sheep. We protect our flocks the old-fashioned way with *Euskal artzain txakurra*."

"That's easy for you to say."

"Basque sheep dogs."

Susannah's family name is Inchaustigui. Her family doesn't speak Basque at home, but she learned some from her grandfather. She says she's not fluent, but how would anyone know?

Basque, or *Euskara* as they call it, is the only remaining language in Europe that predates the Indo-European languages. Some people have speculated that the Basque language evolved from an earlier version spoken by the Neanderthals. I advise you not to mention this theory in the presence of Susannah's brothers if you value your health.

We do know that Basque was being spoken when the Romans invaded, but the people were illiterate, so there is no history of the language. Linguists assume there were other languages spoken in prehistoric Europe, but they died out long before they could be written down. The same thing probably happened to the language of the people of the cliff dwelling above the Rio Doloroso.

I told her Wiley slept for about an hour. He seemed better when he woke up. So I sent Geronimo ahead as scout and followed him. This time Wiley hobbled along behind.

"What about your fear of heights?"

"I forced the rebar through the back of my hat and hung the gunny sack from it like blinders. The only thing I saw until we reached the switchbacks was basalt."

"Basalt?"

"Yeah. The Rio Doloroso flows into the Rio Grande Gorge. But the Rio Grande didn't dig out that gorge the way the Colorado dug the Grand Canyon. The gorge was formed by volcanic action, and all the rivers and streams fell into it by gravity. So the sides of the canyons are mostly the basalt left by eruptions."

"I'm sure this is fascinating to a geologist, but what does it have to do with your escape from the cliff dwelling?"

"Basalt is basically lava. It cracks when it cools, so there were plenty of places to hold on to. I walked sideways facing the cliff and concentrated on handholds."

"If you had on blinders, how did you know you needed to hold on?"

"The need was psychological. I didn't hold on to keep from falling. I held on to keep from having a heart attack. The worst part was right at the end. There's a stack of boulders you have to work around, and they seemed none too stable."

I was happy to see Angie with our refills. Recounting my misadventure had me needing a drink. I took a sip and discovered it was as good as the last one. "I was hoping to see the Bronco when we reached high ground, but all I saw was Cerro Roto."

She did that thing she does where she pushes her shoulders one way and her head another. It means she's confused, but it's becoming in a strange way.

"You heard the Bronco start up and drive away. What part of that made you think it would still be there?"

"I heard it start, but I didn't know how far it was driven. For all I knew it was only a hundred yards away."

"Why would someone drive it a hundred yards and then just leave it there?"

"Here's a better question," I said. "Why would a car thief be where there is no road? Not exactly fertile hunting ground for cars. Here's another good question. How did he get there? It's in the middle of nowhere, so he didn't walk. He probably got there in a four-wheel-drive truck or a jeep. So if he drove the Bronco away, he'd have to leave his own vehicle behind."

"Unless he had a partner in crime."

"That still wouldn't explain what they were doing there or why they would want a beat-up old Bronco. If you rule out car theft, the only explanation for the Bronco being moved is someone moving it just to take my rope away. In that case, all he had to do was drive it a few feet and leave."

She twirled her glass while she considered it. "So it was either a car thief or someone who wanted to strand you."

"Why would a car thief be—"

"You already asked that. There are a thousand answers. He was dove hunting, riding a dirt bike, prospecting for gold. It doesn't really matter. A car thief can be anywhere. And if he happens to come across a car . . . were the keys in it?"

I hesitated. "Yes."

"There's more, isn't there?" She sees right through me.

"It was running."

"You left the engine running while you descended down to the cliff dwelling?"

"The winch draws a lot of current. If the battery died, I wouldn't be able to get back up using the rope, so I left the engine running to keep the battery charged."

"It could have been teenagers pulling a prank."

"Maybe. Despite Alvar telling me that no one knows where the place is, there was evidence of campfires, and not ancient ones."

"Maybe they consider it their secret hiding place," she said. "Kids like to do that. Like the Indian cave in *Dead Poets Society*."

"Having a secret place is fun, but stranding someone in a cliff dwelling is hardly a prank."

"Teenagers don't think straight. It's their hormones."

I watched her sip her margarita while her wheels turned.

"Maybe it was another treasure hunter who didn't want you snooping around his secret pot-hunting place."

She seemed determined to add a second pot hunter to the story, either as the corpse I defiled or as a competitor stealing my truck.

When I didn't comment, she said, "Or an Indian who wanted to punish you for defiling a holy place."

"Or maybe the spirit of the dead guy drove it away," I said.

# 6

Despite my brilliant reasoning, the Bronco was nowhere in sight when we cleared the canyon. We had to walk back to civilization.

Or what passes for civilization in New Mexico.

I took the gunny sack off the rebar and the rebar out of my hat. But even though I was now able to look back, I didn't. I needed to concentrate on getting out.

The surest path would have been retracing the route I took to get there. But that route had taken me over an old low bridge across the Rio Grande and far below the surrounding plateau. After crossing the bridge and maneuvering the narrow switchbacks up the other side, I had left the road and driven thirty miles weaving between dunes, arroyos, lava flows and brush. I had checked the topo map frequently because my primary means of navigation was comparing the contour lines on the map with the ground I was covering. That and judging the sight-line angles to Cerro Roto.

I might have been able to find enough of my tire tracks to follow them back to the road. But it would be slow going in rough terrain. Especially with a wounded coyote in my posse.

It was noon by the time we reached the rim of the Rio Doloroso Canyon. There was no way we could reach the road before dark. We'd have to spend the night on the plateau, reach the road in the morning then spend the rest of the day getting to the Rio Grande.

At which point the trip would become even more challenging. We'd have to descend down a narrow switchback road to the low bridge. I remembered a park ranger saying if the Empire State Building were placed in the Rio Grande Gorge, the mast at the top would be the only thing visible. So you could at least see King Kong if he were up there swatting at planes.

We'd probably arrive around dark. So we'd be making the descent after walking thirty miles and sleeping rough. I wasn't confident we could make the trip on our nine legs. Ten if Wiley's left front one could be depended upon.

Another option would be to head to the Rio Grande Gorge Bridge. Unlike the old low bridge, it spans the gorge at the top so there are no switchbacks and climbs. But it was even farther away. And it's the third highest bridge in the country which was reason enough for an acrophobe like me to avoid it.

Then I remembered looking at the topo map with Alvar Nuñez. We could go to La Reina. It was only twenty miles away, a long hike across rough terrain, but closer than either bridge and also level.

Except the topo map was in the Bronco. I tried to picture it.

The map, that is. I didn't need to picture the Bronco. I knew exactly what it looked like. Which was good because the mental image was the only thing I had to remember it by.

Even the key was gone.

I realized my house key was on the same ring. Great. If by some miracle I made it back to Albuquerque, I'd have to break in to my own home.

If the mental image I concocted of the map was correct, we needed to travel northwest at about 315 degrees. We set off in that direction.

It wasn't long until Wiley was looking haggard.

We stopped to eat. Wiley needed to build up his strength. He got a whole *chorizo*. Geronimo got half of one. I decided it was a perfect time to start that diet I'd been contemplating. I was up to 150, more than my 5' 6" frame is accustomed to.

We made a few miles that afternoon, but it was clear we were going to spend a night on the Rio Grande plateau. At dusk, I found a suitable place for a campsite in a small depression between two juniper trees. I discovered a roadrunner also liked the site when I reached for some dry sticks at the base of one of the junipers and he growled at me.

Yes, growled. They do not go "beep, beep" like the cartoon version. They have quite a vocal repertoire—cooing, clacking, growling, whirling, popping and barking. In this latter respect, they outshine Geronimo.

This particular roadrunner was probably upset that we were in his territory. They mate in the spring, so he wasn't protecting a nest, a task he shares with the female. They are good parents except for the fact that a chick who is sickly will be dismembered and fed to its siblings.

Life can be harsh in the desert.

Roadrunner cartoons are fun, but in real life, coyotes do not chase roadrunners. For one thing, they couldn't catch them.

Which is probably a good thing for the coyote. Roadrunners are fierce. The males draw night hunting duties when chicks are in the nest, so I've seen quite a few when I'm also on midnight hunts. I've witnessed a roadrunner catch a rattlesnake that was trying to strike him. He grabbed the snake's head so he couldn't bite and then whipped the poor reptile back and forth on the ground until the spinal column was shattered and the snake immobilized. I suppose he took it back to the nest, tore it into pieces and fed it to his young.

After lecturing Geronimo about The Native American Graves Protection and Repatriation Act and explaining to Wiley that he had to follow us out of the canyon even if his leg hurt, I was beginning to feel a bit like Dr. Doolittle. So I told the roadrunner (scientific name: *Boulevardius burnupius*) that he'd just have to put up with us because we were too tired to move on.

Dinner was half a *chorizo* for Wiley and a quarter of one for Geronimo. I sprayed some more Bactine on Wiley's leg.

My own dinner was the Euell Gibbons special—some goosefoot seeds, juniper berries and a few piñon nuts. The BLM requires a permit to gather piñon nuts. I'd already committed two felonies by violating ARPA and NAGPRA, so I wasn't much bothered by adding a misdemeanor to my rap sheet for gathering piñon nuts without a permit.

What did bother me was the tooth I broke while splitting the tough outer shells of the piñons.

I found a flat rock with a slight depression in it and tipped in a few tablespoons of water for Geronimo. Then I added a few for Wiley. When Geronimo and I moved away from the rock, Wiley lapped up the water.

I took a sip from the canteen and then rattled it like they do in the old movies to judge how much water was in it. I'm not sure how to convert the sloshing sound to an amount, but it didn't sound like much.

A person can survive about three days without water. I wondered what 'without' meant in this case. Would a few tablespoons a day prolong survival?

I cuddled up with Geronimo for warmth and tried to sleep. I knew my diet was working because my stomach was rumbling. I passed the time I should have been sleeping by wondering whether I could bake goosefoot seeds into griddle cakes as the Zuni traditionally did. I had the fire but lacked a pan. Not to mention enough seeds to make a cake bigger than a dime. I suppose you grind them and mix them with water. I didn't have much of that either.

I awoke shortly before sunup. Wiley was gone. I couldn't blame him. I wasn't providing enough food or water. His chances of survival were better on his own. Nature had equipped him for it.

I was sort of fond of him. He had a bushy tail and a mouth that curved up at the sides so that he seemed to be smiling. I would miss him, but I was happy he was gone. I could give more food and water to Geronimo who, unlike Wiley, was not prepared for survival in the desert.

Unless we found a big ant hill and he could feast on those.

Wiley wasn't the only thing that was gone. My hat was nowhere to be found. Even though it had two holes in it where I had forced the rebar through, I was sorry it was gone. I liked that hat, in part because the label claimed it was "handcrafted with Canadian persnicketiness."

We skipped breakfast and headed out.

At the edge of the depression in which we had spent the night was a mound of damp sand. At the bottom of the hole from which the sand had been excavated was a tiny amount of water. I figured Wiley had dug for water before he left. It would be nice to think he left it for us, but it's more likely that it seeped in after he left. But at least he knew where to dig. I let Geronimo drink it. It wasn't much of a sacrifice—I hate gritty water.

There was no way to know when Wiley had left. Maybe he dug the hole right after I went to sleep, found no water and left. In that case, the water Geronimo had lapped up had taken all night to accumulate. Not worth waiting for.

Or maybe it had all seeped up in just a few minutes. I dug deeper and waited to see if more water would seep in.

One symptom of dehydration is irrationality. Waiting too long for water that might not come could prevent us from reaching La Reina where there was water. But the small amount we had might not be enough to get us there. I tried to stay calm and rational. I decided to give it an hour. No water accumulated. We started walking.

We were well above seven thousand feet. That meant the air was relatively cool. But it also meant the sunlight had less atmosphere to penetrate. Lacking a hat, I draped the gunny sack over my head to protect against the sun. As the day heated up I began to feel like I was under a broiler.

Thirsty people panic and make bad decisions. Like not drinking enough water. Victims of dehydration are sometimes found next to half-full canteens. In their desperate attempt to save water, they dehydrate their brain. Better to take a quenching chug and keep moving than to take sips that only wet your whistle.

We were making better time without Wiley. I wanted to maintain our brisk pace. I wanted to drink enough water to hydrate my brain. I tipped my head back to take a swig from the canteen. My foot caught between two rocks, and I fell on my face.

The canteen clattered away, its precious contents washing over the rocks. At least Geronimo had the good sense to lap up what he could get to.

# 7

"Who is Euell Gibbons?" Susannah asked.

"He was before your time. I liked him because he and I both grew up in New Mexico. During the dust-bowl days when he was just a kid, his father left the family to try to find work. After he'd been gone a few days, the family had eaten everything in the house except some dried pinto beans. Euell went into the wild and came back with piñon nuts, prickly pear fruit and puffball mushrooms. His mother and three siblings survived for a month on the food Euell foraged."

"He told you that?"

I laughed. "I didn't know him. I just knew about him because he was famous for eating wild plants. When I was a kid, he was often a guest on Sonny and Cher or The Tonight Show."

"Eating wild plants got you on television in those days?"

"The back to nature thing was just getting popular, and he had this sort of rustic persona. I remember when Sonny and Cher awarded him a wooden plaque, he took a bite of it."

"Is that how you broke your tooth, trying to eat wood?"

"Nope. Piñon nuts, which are harder than wood."

"And the sunburn?"

"My hat disappeared. Maybe it blew away during the night. Or maybe Geronimo ate it. He was hungry enough to do so."

"And you got the black eye and skinned nose when you tried to walk and drink at the same time."

I admitted it.

Susannah doesn't have classes on Friday night, which was a good thing since my cliff dwelling narrative was taking longer than the 3,182 alliterative lines of *Beowulf*.

I waved Angie over and asked for a large glass of ice water. I still felt dehydrated. And I wanted to limit my alcohol intake. Two margaritas were enough for a man in my condition.

Susannah asked for more salsa then turned to me. "Are you going to tell me what finally happened, or do you want me to piece together the story by your appearance? Your lips are scabs. Your nose is glowing like a stop light. You have a black eye and a broken tooth. You have a cast on your ankle, and you've been squinting all evening."

"And those are my best features."

I sipped some water while she laughed. "Oddly enough, the first thing I did after the fall was check the shard. I had it in my shirt pocket. It was so long that it stuck out, so I couldn't button the pocket. I was relieved to see it wasn't broken."

"I'm not surprised you checked the shard before you checked your ankle. You treat that stuff like it's holy."

"Maybe it is. But this one is strange."

"How so?"

"I'm not sure exactly. Something about the design."

"Like you think you've seen it before?"

"No. What bothers me is that I *haven't* seen it before. But I don't know why that bothers me. It's not like I know every design ever made by ancient potters."

"Maybe it will come to you when you try to make a copy based on the shard."

I suspected she was right. That often happens.

"I finally managed to stand up. But when I put weight on the bad ankle, I collapsed again. The pain was severe. I knew I wasn't going to be able to walk. I tried to convince Geronimo to go for help, but he didn't understand."

"Why am I not surprised? Then what?"

"I started thinking about dying."

"Wow," she said slowly, drawing the word out into two syllables like she really meant it. "Were you scared?"

"Not at first. I didn't want to die, of course, but I figured I was luckier than most people. I had great parents and a happy childhood. I've had good health and good friends. And dying of thirst is not gruesome or painful. I told myself there are lots of worse ways to go. Then I looked up and thought I was headed for one of those worse ways. A guy was walking towards me with a hunting bow in his right hand and a bloody dead body thrown over his left shoulder."

"Let me guess. He also had war paint on his face and feathers in his hair. The dehydration was causing you to hallucinate."

"He wasn't wearing a headdress, just a wide-brimmed hat. He knew better than to go out in the New Mexico sun without a hat because he was a doctor."

"And the bloody guy was one of his patients?"

"No, when they got closer, I realized he was part of an elk. Or *it* was part of an elk. The doctor had killed it and was hauling it back to a Jeep. His name is Fred Koelher. He checked to make sure I didn't need immediate attention then dropped the elk piece and jogged away. He returned a few minutes later in the Jeep with his guide, a hulking man with dark eyes whom he introduced as Alonso Castillo Maldonado."

"Koehler gave you the first, last and middle names of his guide? That's sort of formal when you're meeting out in the wild, isn't it?"

"He didn't give me a middle name because the guide didn't have one. 'Castillo' and 'Maldonado' are his two last names."

"Two things can't both be last, Hubert."

I thought about that for a few seconds. "You're right. In Spanish they're called *apellidos*, what I guess we would call 'appellations'. It's the way people have traditionally been named in Spain, and the tradition came here with the *conquistadores*. A person's first *apellido* is his father's name."

"Shouldn't you say 'his or hers'?"

"I said 'his' because the person we happen to be discussing is a man. But women are actually more important in the Spanish naming system. The second *apellido* comes from the mother, the third from the paternal grandmother, the fourth from the maternal grandmother, the fifth from the—"

"Okay, I get it. All the names except the first one come from women. How many can they have?"

"I guess since they expelled the Moslem invaders, they can have only one woman."

"Sheesh. How many *names*?"

"So far as I know, the sky's the limit for *apellidos*. Most people these days just use two. So the doctor should have introduced the guide as Alonso Castillo. But he probably didn't know that and was just trying to be polite."

"Shouldn't he have introduced him as Alonso Maldonado?"

"No, when you address someone, you always use the first last name."

"Nothing can be a *first* last name. If it's really last, then it's the *only* last name."

"Right again. I should have said the first *apellido*. Guess where Castillo lives?"

"In Maldonado?"

"That's a good one. No, he lives in La Reina. Some coincidence, right?"

"There are no coincidences, Hubert."

"So you always say."

"And even if there were coincidences, that wouldn't be one."

I didn't argue the point. I didn't even understand it.

"They lifted me into the Jeep and took me to Taos. Then Dr. Koehler took me from there to Albuquerque in his rental car."

"Rental car?"

"Yeah, he lives back east, but he comes out here every year to hunt elk. That's probably why he didn't understand the Spanish naming custom."

"Hunting elk makes you misunderstand Spanish names?"

I made no reply.

"Anyway," she said, "you were right about being luckier than most people. There you were in the middle of nowhere, miles from a road and on the verge of death, and a doctor comes along and takes you home. I guess he put that cast on your ankle, too."

"He did."

I gave her a sly smile. "But I'm not all that lucky."

"Okay," she said resignedly, "I'll play the straight man. Why are you not all that lucky?"

"Because I had to ride two hours in a Jeep with part of a dead elk in my lap. Then I couldn't get into my house because my house key was on the key ring in the Bronco. And to top it all off, Koehler charged me to set my ankle."

"How did you get into your house?"

"Koehler used his cell phone to call Tristan. Remember he installed that electronic lock on my shop door? I have a remote that unlocks it. Of course the remote was inside, but Tristan had anticipated I might misplace or break it, so he had a back-up."

"But the door from the shop back to your studio and house has a dead bolt."

"Once I got into the shop, I called a locksmith. After he let me into my workshop, the doc did the cast."

"How much did he charge?"

"The locksmith charged two hundred. Koehler only charged one hundred."

"That's a bargain, Hubie. If you'd gone to the emergency room, it would probably have been five hundred."

"Maybe, but he didn't even have to pay for materials. He used gauze from my first aid kit to wrap the ankle and my potting clay to form the cast."

"I wondered why it was brown. You want me to sign it?"

# 8

"What are you doing for your sunburn," Sharice asked.

"Nuffing. I em tying u maa mah shin looh lie yuz," I replied.

"Why would you want your skin to look like mine?"

I'm always amazed she understands what I'm saying even when I'm shot full of Novocain and have cotton wads between my gums and cheeks. Maybe it's a skill hygienists acquire from years of listening to dental chair babble.

I wanted to tell her it's because her sepia skin is so matte that nothing reflects from it. But that's the sort of thing you say over candlelight in a restaurant. It loses most of its magic when the person you're saying it to is wiping drool off your face.

Dr. Batres returned to remove the clamp from my repaired tooth. After a little polishing, he pronounced it both functionally and cosmetically perfect. Sharice held a mirror in front of my face, but I was enjoying looking at her, so I passed up the opportunity to admire the doc's handwork. He was a little too self-satisfied in my opinion. He lists himself as Dr. Batres, D.M.D, putting one form of 'doctor' before his name and another form after it. Seems like overkill to me.

I was already dreading the bill.

Sharice removed my bib and gave me a plastic bag with a travel-sized tube of toothpaste, a spool of floss and a bright orange tooth-brush. Four hundred dollars for twenty minutes work, and they think a dollar bag of dental supplies makes the expense easier to swallow.

"Do you have a toothbrush that doesn't glow in the dark?" I asked her.

I did want a tamer color, but the real reason I asked was to see if removing the clip and the cotton had improved my enunciation. It had, so I asked Sharice if she would have dinner with me, and she said yes.

Sharice and I have been casually flirting with each other for two or three years. Actually, she does most of the flirting. It's hard to reciprocate with her fingers in my mouth, although I suppose under other circumstances that could be a form of flirting. We had lunch together once, not really a date. It turned out to be fun, so I asked her out. But she said her boyfriend wouldn't approve. After my next appointment, she said she didn't have her boyfriend anymore. I was seeing Dolly then, so nothing came of it.

Not counting the few times a year I have to crawl because I've had too much to drink, I have two means of getting around. I walk and I drive my Bronco. Since neither of those options was now available, I had enlisted Tristan to drive me to the dentist.

The receptionist was flirting with him when I returned to the waiting room. He has olive skin, thick dark hair that hangs down in ringlets and what most girls seem to think of as bed-room eyes. He's also a considerate person, which is even rarer among men than being handsome.

He's not really my nephew. He's the grandson of my great aunt Beatrice. I don't know what that makes him kinship-wise, but he seems like a nephew, so that's what I call him.

He handed me my crutches and laughed as I struggled through the door.

"You're not exactly adept with those."

"I've never been athletic," I said

"Using crutches isn't a sport."

"Sure it is. Haven't you heard of the Special Olympics?"

As we headed for the parking lot, he asked to see the tooth. I curled back my lips.

"I liked your look better with the chipped tooth. It sort of fit with the treasure hunter image."

"Thanks, I think. Sharice must like the toothpaste ad look. She agreed to have dinner with me Saturday night. And I noticed the receptionist had her eyes on you. I guess the dentist's office is where the Schuze men go to meet chicks."

"Nobody says 'chicks' anymore, Uncle Hubert. And what about Dolly?"

"She dumped me the morning I left for that ill-fated event at the D. H. Lawrence Ranch."

"Even though all your teeth were good at that point? Why did she dump you?"

The truth is I had no idea. I met Dolly Madison Aguirre when I was going door to door pretending to be a volunteer at the animal shelter. What I was *really* trying to do was locate a house where I had appraised a collection of ancient pots. I had to see inside the house to identify it because seeing the exterior was no help. I had arrived and departed wearing a blindfold.

Don't ask.

Geronimo played the role of the dog whose owner I was trying to find. I thought we made a convincing team, but the scam went sour when Dolly said she wanted to adopt Geronimo if his owner couldn't be found.

I should have just moved on to the next house and forgotten her. But I returned the next day for a reason just as bizarre as the first visit, and we ended up dating. Turns out her father had been my high school history teacher. She told me after a few months that she had been unlucky in marriage and didn't want to try it again, thus fending off a proposal which I may or may not have made.

I thought about this as we crossed the parking lot to Tristan's car.

"She said she dumped me because I was taking Susannah to the Lawrence Ranch as my girlfriend."

He turned to look at me. "But she knew you and Susannah are just friends."

"And when I reminded her of that, she said the real reason was I stole her dog."

"Geronimo was her dog?"

So I had to tell him about the ruse I used with Geronimo as a lost dog. "When she came to my house the first time, she saw Geronimo was still there. She seemed to take it well. She said I had seen him first and therefore had first claim on him. The subject never came up again until she accused me of stealing him from her. But at that point her behavior had been erratic for weeks, so I don't think that was the real reason."

"Erratic how?"

"She seemed stable all through the first months of our relationship. Then she became moody and argumentative. She would blow up at the smallest thing. Then she would cool down and apologize. Then she would lose it again ten minutes later. Maybe she had allergies or a bad reaction to something. She was always complaining of being too hot."

He started laughing. "And you never figured it out?"

"Figured what out?"

"Mood swings. Hot flashes. It's called menopause, Uncle Hubert."

"And you know about this how?"

"Everybody knows about it. There are even ads on television."

"Menopause advertises?"

"Well, not menopause exactly, but medicines for it."

"So they found a cure?"

He laughed again. "It's not a disease. It's a natural transition women go through. But there are medicines for the unpleasant symptoms like hot flashes and mood swings."

"And they talk about that on television?"

"Sure. And constipation, warts and erectile dysfunction."

Another reason not to watch television, I thought to myself.

"Where to now," he asked, "a car dealer?"

"I've decided I don't need a car. Walking is good for me and good for the planet."

He glanced at me. "It's Albuquerque, Uncle Hubert. Two hundred square miles of city and about a hundred yards of sidewalk."

"Most of them in my neighborhood."

"And how will you pick up Sharice Saturday night?"

"I couldn't pick her up in a car even if I had one. I can't drive until the cast comes off."

"How long will that be?"

"Six weeks. In the meantime, Dr. Koehler recommended RICE, but I don't see how I can do that."

"Why not, you like rice."

"Not the grain. It's an acronym for rest, ice, compression and elevation. But I can't rest because I can't get comfortable with this thing on my leg. I can't ice it either. When I stuck my foot in a tub of ice, my toes got cold but my ankle didn't. I think the cast insulates too well. I can't compress my ankle with the cast on it, so the only one I can really use is elevation."

"Lucky for you Albuquerque is over five thousand feet."

I laughed.

He looked down at the cast and asked, "You want me to sign it?"

# 9

After Tristan dropped me off in the alley, I hobbled into my living quarters looking for something to read before opening for the afternoon rush, an event that lives more in hope than in reality.

The only thing on hand was *Ben-Hur* which I had checked out from the library along with *The Wooing of Malkatoon*. I went to the shop, rotated the sign to 'Open' and started reading in the hope that the *Ben-Hur* would be better than *Malkatoon*.

It was a reasonable prospect. According to the dust jacket, *Ben-Hur* was the best-selling novel of the nineteenth century, surpassing Harriet Beecher Stowe's *Uncle Tom's Cabin*. And it remained the best-selling book until it was topped by Margaret Mitchell's *Gone with the Wind* in the 1930s. When the film version of *Ben-Hur* won eleven Academy Awards in 1959, sales of the book soared, and it went back in front of *Gone with the Wind*.

I guess people liked the movie so much that they ran out and bought the book. But I wonder how many people actually read the entire thing.

In my case, I made it only to the end of the first paragraph. There Wallace describes the mountain named *Jebel es Zubleh*:

> Its feet are well covered by sands tossed from the Euphrates, there to lie, for the mountain is a wall to the pasture-lands of Moab and Ammon on the west—lands which else had been of the desert a part.

"Tossed from the Euphrates, there to lie"?

"Of the desert a part"?

Who knew that Lew Wallace was the inspiration for Yoda?

Finish *Ben-Hur* I could not.

But while the book was dreadful, the publisher's introduction was fascinating. Wallace completed the novel at what he called "my rough pine-table" in his room in the Palace of the Governors in Santa Fe. He said in his memoir that he wrote the final scenes by lantern light after returning from a clandestine meeting with Henry McCarty, also known as Henry Antrim and William H. Bonney.

But best known as Billy the Kid.

I wondered why Wallace and Billy the Kid met. I wondered how Wallace could segue from a meeting with a notorious outlaw to putting the finishing touches on a book subtitled *A Tale of the Christ*.

My wonderings were interrupted by the bong sound that indicates someone passing through my door. I looked up hoping to see the beginning of the afternoon rush. I was badly in need of money. The thousand I'd paid to Alvar had depleted my stash. I'd paid two hundred to the locksmith and a hundred to Dr. Koehler. The crutches were fifteen a week. I had a four-hundred-dollar dental bill and despite what I'd told Tristan, I knew I'd eventually have to buy a car.

But it was not a rush. It wasn't even a customer. It was Miss Gladys Claiborne, proprietor of the eponymous Miss Gladys' Gift Shop, an emporium two doors from my own.

You're not supposed to eat before going to the dentist, and hobbling burns more energy than you might expect. So I was hungry enough to eat one of Miss Gladys' casseroles of doom.

Which was a good thing because that's what she had brought.

Before serving the casserole, she asked about my ankle.

She knows about my pot hunting, but I didn't want to distress her by talking about the body I'd found so I just said I was out looking for pots and strained my ankle when it caught between two rocks.

"I don't believe I've ever seen a beige cast," she said.

"The doctor used my potting clay. I like to think of it as one of my pots on my foot."

"That's very clever of you. Can I sign it?"

Miss Gladys is a good friend and good neighbor. Her dedication to keeping me well fed has made me an expert on her casseroles which fall into two categories: savory and sweet. The savory ones have five ingredients—a meat, a starch, veggies, cheese and the glue that holds everything together. The glue is usually Campbell's Cream of Fill-In-The-Blank.

"I've decided to go international," she announced as she spread a placemat on my counter and positioned a plate, silverware and tall glass on it. She approves of neither paper plates nor plastic utensils. The embroidered bags she uses to transport these meals are made of sturdy canvas, and I marvel that she can lift them.

"I got the recipe for this dolmades casserole from Prissy Papas. Her real first name is Aphrodite, but she didn't like the way people in Texas shortened her Greek name to the first two syllables, so she insisted we call her Prissy."

She paused for a moment and put her pointing finger against the dimple in her cheek. "Now that I think on it, 'Prissy' fit her better than 'Aphrodite'. Anyway, she is a genuine Greek. Her grandfather's name was Papadimitropoulos. She and two of her brothers, Peter and Andrew, shortened it to Papas."

"Who could blame them?"

"Another brother, Harry, used Tropolos. Nicholas refused to shorten it, so the family gave him the nickname 'Enchilada' which was short for 'the whole enchilada' because the name was so long."

"So Nicholas was the only one with a *nick* name," I quipped, but she didn't get it.

"So far as I know. The grandfather came straight from Athens to Port Arthur and worked in the refineries until he had enough money to start a restaurant."

Miss Gladys' explanations of her casseroles often include more information about the person who invented them than about the ingredients. I've found that asking questions merely delays the inevitable, so I usually just nod and smile.

It turned out that the meat, starch, veggies, cheese and glue in this case were, respectively, ground beef, rice, grape leaves, feta and Campbell's Cream of Chicken Soup.

I didn't know grape leaves were a veggie. The feta made the dish a bit salty, but it was otherwise tasty, and I told her so. I was thinking if I dropped the feta and added chopped jalapeños and cilantro, it might be worth making. Casseroles create leftovers, but Tristan will eat anything, so . . .

"I see you're reading *Ben-Hur*," she said, snapping me out of my speculations on casseroles. "My church group studied that last year. What do you think of it?"

"I haven't finished it."

"Then you have a treat in store for you."

"How so?"

She looked up at me with those twinkly blue eyes. "I don't want to spoil it for you."

"That's okay. I think a summary would help." Especially since I'm not going to read the thing, I thought to myself.

She poured me some sweet tea.

"It's a story of two boys living in Jerusalem during the time of Jesus, a Jewish one named Ben-Hur and a Roman one named Messala. I know this makes me seem simple, but I found it helpful to think of them as Tom Sawyer and Huckleberry Finn."

"So it reminded you of Mark Twain?"

"Only the two boys. The writing was much more serious."

That's one word for it, I thought.

"Despite their differences, they were fast friends. Messala eventually becomes a bigwig in the Roman army and is sent back to Jerusalem to make sure the Jews don't revolt against Roman rule. They try to keep politics out of their friendship, but when Messala asks Ben-Hur to help him keep the Jews in line, Ben-Hur says he wants freedom for his people. Messala trumps up some charge against his former friend and sends him off to be one of those poor souls who is chained to an oar and made to row a Roman warship. Did you ever see the movie?"

"I did."

"Then you surely remember the scene where the ship's commander unchains Ben-Hur before the big battle. When the ship is rammed and water floods the compartment where the rowers are, Ben-Hur is able to escape since he's not chained to the ship. He sees the commander drowning because his heavy armor is pulling him down. But Ben-Hur saves him. Isn't that just about the most heartwarming story you ever heard?"

"In what way?"

"Don't you see? Because the commander saved a life, his is saved in return."

I wondered how much moral credit someone who chains a person deserves for later releasing him, but I kept that question to myself.

# 10

"You've barely touched your margarita."

"I had two helpings of a dolmades casserole."

"Miss Gladys?"

"Yeah. She's going international."

"And the source of this dish?"

"Prissy Papas."

She giggled. "That sounds like a name for a fancy Mexican potato dish."

"There were no potatoes in it."

"Let me guess what it did have—ground lamb, rice, grape leaves, feta and raisins."

Susannah knows Miss Gladys' cooking almost as well as I do.

"Close. It didn't have raisins, and it had ground beef instead of lamb. Which is a good thing because I hate lamb."

"You've never even tasted lamb," she retorted.

"I've never tasted bear either, but I know I hate it."

"But you like goat."

"That's different."

"The only difference is that you grew up around people who eat goat. If you'd grown up in a Basque family like me, you'd like lamb."

I had to admit she was right. I've formulated over the years a set of theses, each of which I call a Schuze Anthropological Premise or SAP, which is also what some people think I am for believing them. SAP number 1 is that any human being can practice any culture.

Culture is not biological. It is learned. The dead guy in the cliff dwelling above the Rio Doloroso ate coyotes and gophers. If he had been born near the Bering Sea, he would have eaten whale and seal.

Susannah ordered another margarita. I declined.

"Are you not drinking because of the casserole or is the real reason that your new tooth is sensitive to the cold?"

"It's not a new tooth, just a repair to the chipped one."

"I liked your snaggletoothed look. It worked well with the sunburn, the skinned nose and the cast."

"Tristan said it fit my pot thief image."

"Maybe you should have left it that way."

"Especially since I don't have the money to pay for it. But I don't think it would be acceptable for a dental hygienist to be seen with a snaggletoothed man."

She gave me one of her big rancher-girl smiles. "You finally have a date with Sharice?"

I returned her smile. "This Saturday."

"That's great. You haven't had a date since Dolly dumped you."

"That was your fault, remember? She was jealous of you."

"No, it was because you stole her dog."

Our laughing made me feel better.

I took a sip of my margarita, but it was watered down from sitting there so long.

"The truth is," I said, suddenly in a serious mood, "It was neither you nor Geronimo. It was me. I was too dense to realize she was going through menopause. I should have tried harder to be understanding."

"How do you know she was going through menopause?"

"Tristan told me."

She looked astonished. "Dolly told Tristan she was going through the change?"

"No. He figured it out when I told him this morning about her moodiness and her complaining about being hot. But I told you about her strange behavior months ago. You didn't get it, and you're a woman."

"I'm not a woman, Hubie. I'm a *neskato*. That's what my grandfather always called me. It means 'maiden'. You know—inexperienced."

I knew better than to comment on that, so I told her about my money woes.

"You could go back to that cliff dwelling above the Rio Doloroso. All it would take is one good pot to balance your budget."

"I'm not a grave robber."

"You wouldn't be robbing a grave. You said you marked the grave with that stone, so just dig somewhere else. Surely there's not another body at that site."

"Hmm. You don't think it would be wrong to dig close to a grave?"

"You told me it wasn't a grave. And it makes sense that they wouldn't bury their dead where they lived."

"Okay, it's not a formal grave. But his body is there, and it seems

. . . maybe not ghoulish, because I wouldn't be digging him up, but maybe . . . I don't know, disrespectful?"

We sat in silence while we thought about it.

"Maybe you should move him," she finally said.

"No way. It was bad enough to find him in the first place. And to actually touch his hand with the hole in it."

I shuddered at the memory.

"Maybe digging there is not disrespectful," she said. "But leaving him there might be. Maybe he should have a proper burial."

I shook my head. The whole idea was crazy.

"I already thought of that when I pushed the dirt back and placed the rock over him. I was going to make a cross from two sticks and jam it into the soil behind the rock. Then it dawned on me that he was obviously not a Christian."

"Why not?" she joked, "you just told me he had a hole in his hand like Jesus." She started to laugh at her little joke then bolted upright. "What do you mean he had a hole in his hand?"

"I told you about that. I was probing with my rebar and—"

"But I assumed it just touched his hand. I didn't think it made a hole."

I remembered I hadn't told her that part in detail because it was so disagreeable, and I was ashamed of it to boot.

"I didn't think I had pushed hard enough to penetrate a hand. You know how careful I am. I'd feel awful if I broke a piece of ancient pottery. So I was shocked when I grasped the hand and felt a hole."

"Where was the hole?"

You've probably already figured out where this is headed, but I was still in a fog.

Her question seemed odd. "Like I said, it was in his hand."

"But *where* in his hand?"

"I didn't look. As soon as I realized it was a hand, I dropped it like a burning coal."

The look in her eyes was beginning to worry me. Her stare made me feel like there was something spooky about me.

She spoke slowly. "A thousand-year-old corpse can't have a hole in its hand. It's nothing but a skeleton."

My own hand went to my mouth. The dolmades casserole was threatening to make an unscheduled and highly unpleasant public appearance. I swallowed hard.

After the grape leaf concoction settled down, I drank some of my margarita.

"I need one with more tequila in it," I said and signaled for a refill.

# 11

"I can't believe you didn't realize the hand had flesh on it."

"I told you I dropped it like a hot coal. It was a dark night, and the hand had cold hard fingers. I didn't stop to ask myself whether they were plain bone or bone with dried flesh on them."

"But what about the hole?"

"It was in the ground," I said, hoping to lighten the conversation. She rolled her eyes. "The hole in the hand."

"It must have been in the palm."

"Jeez, Hubert. How can you drop a hand like a hot coal and still have felt both the fingers and the palm?"

"It was like an accidental handshake. When I reached into the excavation, his fingers slid along mine and mine along his. Except for my middle finger that caught in the hole."

"I guess I can see why you didn't know if the fingers were just bone, but didn't it dawn on you that the palm didn't feel like a skeleton?"

"How would I know what a skeleton palm feels like?"

"Well, I'm pretty sure it wouldn't feel like a normal one."

I had to admit she might be right. If so, that meant I might not have violated the Native American Graves Protection and Repatriation Act. If the body was not ancient, it may not have been a Native American. The guy I thought had eaten coyotes and gophers may have had a burger and fries for his last meal.

But who was it? And what era did he come from?

The same questions were occurring to Susannah. "How long does it take the flesh to rot off a buried body?" she asked.

"Can we change the subject, please? I want to forget the dead body, not analyze its decomposition."

The forced remembrance of unearthing a corpse had my stomach churning, but the fresh margarita was moderating my anxiety.

"You can't forget it, Hubert. It may be a murder victim. You have to report it to the police."

Here we go again, I thought to myself. She wants to turn this into a murder mystery.

"The guy I found was not murdered, Susannah. A murderer would have to be crazy to drag a dead body down those steep switchbacks and along the narrow ledge to bury it in a ruin. It would be easier and safer just to throw the body into the gorge."

"Someone might find it in the gorge."

"So what? The corpse isn't going to sit up and announce who killed it."

Her big brown eyes lit up. "A bullet hole! That's what the hole was—a bullet hole."

"A bullet through the hand isn't fatal."

"That's just the first bullet. If you read more murder mysteries, you'd know that. When the murderer aims his gun, the victim's natural response is to stick up his hand in self defense."

She illustrated by extended her arm out in front of her, palm forward. I suppose the feigned fright on her face was to add a dash of drama.

"It's the second bullet that kills. If your digging had been a foot or two in a different direction, you might have felt a hole in his chest instead of his hand."

"Gee, I guess I should feel lucky I only poked a hole in his hand instead of driving the rebar through his heart like I was trying to kill a vampire."

"Sarcasm won't help, Hubert."

I sighed. "I wish it were a bullet hole. Then I wouldn't feel so bad about what happened. But it wasn't a bullet hole. It was the same diameter as my rebar. Face it—I poked a hole in a dead body."

"You must have dropped that hand like a lukewarm coal instead of a hot one, Hubert. You not only felt the fingers and the palm, you also measured the diameter of the hole."

"I didn't measure it. My middle finger fit in it, and my middle finger is about the diameter of the rebar."

"But you were pushing the rebar gently."

"Like I always do."

"So how could it poke a hole?"

I took another sip of my drink. I didn't want this one to get watered down like the first one.

"Okay," I relented. "Maybe the rebar didn't make the hole. But I don't think a bullet made it either."

"What, it was a birth defect?"

"Maybe it was one of those piercings young people seem so fond of these days. Maybe there was a tattoo around the edge of it. Who knows?"

"I do. It was a bullet hole because your rebar couldn't punch a hole in a skeleton."

"Maybe it could. I remember seeing a mummy in the Maxwell Museum of Anthropology at the University. It still had skin on it, and it looked paper thin and brittle."

"Did the palm you touched feel brittle?"

"It didn't occur to me to check whether he needed some Jergens. And it's not my problem."

"Sorry, Hubie, but it is your problem. You found a modern dead person, not an ancient mummy. You have to report it to the police."

Congress may have labeled me a pot thief, but I always try to do the right thing. If it was a modern person—murdered or not—I had a duty to tell someone. But I still thought it was one of the ancient ones. It just didn't make sense that a modern person would be buried that deep in that location. Unless . . .

"Maybe he was officially buried there," I blurted out.

"Huh?"

"Maybe he was an Indian who felt a special kinship with that place and requested to be buried there."

"That is so lame. You'll come up with any excuse to avoid telling the police."

"There's no reason to tell them if it was a planned burial."

"Who gets buried in an ancient cliff dwelling?"

"People specify all sorts of weird places to be buried. Some get buried in a pet cemetery next to their cat or dog. A Beverly Hills woman named Ilene West was buried in her powder blue Ferrari. Her will specified that the seat be reclined to a comfortable angle."

"Well she wouldn't want to spend eternity with the seat at an uncomfortable angle, would she? But that's Beverly Hills. We're talking about the real world here."

"No, Suze, we're talking about New Mexico. There is weird stuff here, too."

"Such as?"

"Well, Carrizozo passed an ordinance making it illegal for a female to appear unshaven in public. And don't forget about the aliens in Roswell."

"Where do you come up with this stuff?"

"I've been reading all about our state because it's the centennial year."

She shook her head. "Let's get back to the subject. Are you going to tell the police about finding the dead guy?"

"I'll send them an anonymous letter telling them exactly where the body is. They can dig it up and do whatever they need to do."

She was shaking her head while I was talking. "Not good enough. They'll need to question you."

"No they won't. I'll include everything in the letter."

"You don't even know what everything *is*. They may have questions that wouldn't occur to you to answer. You have to do this in person."

"You can be very irritating, you know that?"

She gave me another rancher-girl smile. "What else are good friends for?"

"Going to the police will get me in trouble."

"Because you were breaking the Archaeological Resources Protection Act when you found the body."

I nodded.

"How much trouble can that be? You didn't carry anything away."

"Actually, I did. I found that shard before I found the dead guy."

"Nobody cares about shards, Hubie. Our sheep and cattle tromp over them every day. The whole state is littered with them."

"You know I agree with you, but the Feds don't look at it that way."

"So don't say anything about the shard. No one but me knows you took it."

I shook my head. "Two other people know—Dr. Fred Koehler and Alonso Castillo Maldonado."

"Why would you tell the doctor and his hunting guide you took a shard?"

"I didn't tell them. It was sticking out of my pocket, remember?"

"You think they even noticed?"

"Castillo was staring at me."

"What about the doctor?"

"No, he wasn't staring at the doctor."

"You know what I mean."

"I don't know if Koehler noticed the shard, but we were together in the front seat of his rental car for three hours and in my house for another hour while he set my ankle. Incidentally, he's a big fan of Billy the Kid and has read everything ever written about him."

"Well even if he did see the shard, he's back home now. Do you think Castillo was staring at the shard because he's an Indian and was upset that you had it?"

"I don't think he's an Indian. He had a thick beard. And I don't know for sure that it was the shard he was staring at. Maybe he just liked my shirt with the button-flap pockets."

"I don't think it matters. How would the Feds know to ask Castillo whether you took anything? They won't even know you two ever met."

She was right, of course. But I still had a problem. "Just the digging is illegal even if you don't find anything. And the punishment for first-time offenders is a fine of up to $20,000 and a prison term of up to a year."

"It might be worse for you because you aren't a first-time offender."

"Actually, I'd be considered one because I've never been caught."

I thought about the rest of the law—I know it well—and laughed.

"What's so funny?"

"ARPA also allows the Feds to confiscate any vehicles used in the violation. Maybe I could strike a plea bargain with them to just take the Bronco and not give me a prison term."

"But the Bronco is gone."

"Precisely. If they can find it, they can have it."

# 12

I was missing my mother.

There, I said it. It's not that easy for a guy to do. Sentiment is soluble in testosterone.

She passed away on the last day of the twentieth century. Mom was an idealistic person who devoted much of her considerable energy to promoting civility. She was in poor health the last year of her life. I like to think she chose to die on December 31st, 1999 because she didn't want to know what the new millennium would bring.

I'm fortunate to have a sort of second mother, a nanny who arrived in the Schuze household the day my mother brought me home from the maternity ward. I learned Spanish from Consuela, not by lessons but by the method children naturally learn a language, having her speak to me in that tongue from the time I was an infant. My mother was happy I grew up bilingual even though she herself never made any attempt to learn Spanish.

Consuela left to get married the year I started college, and she and Emilio eventually ended up living in Albuquerque's South Valley in a modest adobe home surrounded by pecan trees. The urban sprawl has almost reached them, but for now it remains a pastoral setting.

Emilio and Consuela have one daughter, Ninfa, who is now short one kidney because she was the donor for her mother's recent transplant. I had volunteered to be the donor but neither my blood nor my tissue samples were a match.

But my wallet was. The money I paid for the 'patient responsibility' portion of the bill would have come in handy now that I was broke, but it was money well spent.

And money neither Emilio nor Consuela knew I spent. They think my parents provided them with health insurance. And I guess in a way they did—me. So when someone criticizes what I do for a living, it doesn't bother me. It's not like I use my income from purloined pots to buy Ferraris and Rolexes.

No big sacrifice. I'd be afraid to drive a Ferrari and I don't care what time it is.

I was under the pecan trees on Saturday morning drinking coffee and eating *marranitos*, spicy little gingerbread pigs. These pigs are perfectly kosher. It is their shape, not their ingredients, that give rise to the name. The scent of the spices from Consuela's kitchen tugged me back to my childhood.

"I will bring more *marranitos*," Consuela said, starting to rise from her chair.

I raised a hand like a white flag. "*Gracias, pero no*. I've had too many already."

"But you are too skinny."

She thinks a man in his forties should have a bulge here and there, a sign of health and contentment. I had looked that way before venturing out to the Rio Doloroso, but I'd lost four pounds before I was rescued.

Then I gained twice that much in the first hour after I got home. That was because Dr. Koehler put an eight pound cast on my ankle. I figured dragging that weight around would help me lose more weight. And I was also cutting back on the margaritas.

Consuela subscribes to the *dicho* that a good husband should be *feo, formal y fuerte*. Although the literal meaning is ugly, formal and strong, what those words mean in the *dicho* is more like masculine, stable and stalwart, an exact description of Emilio.

I usually get all the exercise I need by walking, but I had used city buses for this visit, the number 54 from downtown south on 4th, right on Bridge, across the river and south on Coors. I changed to the 155 at the bus stop near the intersection with Arenal and continued even further south almost to Gun Club Road.

Emilio met me at the road, and I hobbled down the dirt lane with my rental crutches and his assistance. Tristan was right. I had to buy a vehicle.

I had spent the night wrestling with my conscience instead of sleeping. Should I do nothing? I didn't think the dead guy was modern, and I certainly didn't think he'd been murdered.

But I couldn't be sure.

So why not just send an anonymous letter? Susannah's argument that I might leave something out was not convincing. Once the police dug the guy up, they could find out everything they needed to know.

Maybe.

The only thing I was certain about was I didn't want to go to prison.

Sitting under the trees with the sun just starting to peek over the

Sandias, the smell of irrigated soil in the air and a warm *marranito* in my hand was just what I needed to relax. And maybe get some advice.

"Your leg, it is broken?" asked Emilio.

"Only sprained."

"Sprained?"

"*Esguince.*"

"Ah. Is worse than broken."

"I never see you sunburned before," said Consuela.

So I told them about my adventure on the Rio Doloroso.

When I got to the part about the dead person, Consuela crossed herself and said, "This is very sad. He is forever alone."

"I guess all dead people are alone," I said.

She shook her head. "No. We visit them each year on *El Día de los Muertos*. We clean and decorate the graves and bring *ofrendas* such as *dulces*, tequila and of course *pan de muerto* and *cempasúchil*."

"You know what is *cempasúchil*, Huberto?" Emilio asked.

"*Claro*. It was originally a wreath of twenty flowers that we call marigolds in English. The Aztecs called them the flowers of death."

"*Bravo*," he said and patted my shoulder.

Consuela said, "Someone must move this man so that his family can visit him."

I was afraid I knew who that someone would be. As unsavory as the idea was to me, only one line of action satisfied my conscience. I had to return to the cliff dwelling and look at that hand. If it was the hand of a prehistoric person, I would leave him to rest in peace. He had no family who would visit.

If it was a contemporary corpse, I would go to the police in person.

It was risky business. Unless I bought another vehicle with a winch and repeated my rope trick, I'd have to wind down those switchbacks and creep along the precipice, a terrifying prospect. I'd have to dig in a grave and examine the hand of a dead person close enough to be sure if it was ancient or modern. And finally, I'd be risking a prison term.

I didn't think it would come to that. After all, I would surely get some credit for reporting the body. And I hadn't taken anything except the shard which only Koehler and Castillo knew about, and neither of them would know I had gone to the police. But prison was a possibility.

Although I decided that doing the right thing was worth facing my fear of heights, breaking my code of never digging in a grave and even going to prison, I don't want to leave you with the impression that my motivation was totally pure and noble.

There was also an upside.

If I was going to put fear, principle and prison on the line, I figured I might as well do a little prospecting before I dug up the hand.

# 13

Clambering onto the bus back to town with crutches was awkward, but the riders were understanding and friendly, so once I was aboard, I enjoyed the ride.

There's a sort of democracy to public transportation, everyone paying the same fare and sitting on the same uncomfortable molded-plastic seats. Strangers become instant comrades. A woman next to me asked in halting English how I injured my leg. I answered in Spanish that I had fallen down while drinking water, and everyone around us laughed. When she got off at the next stop she said goodbye as if she expected to see me the next afternoon.

I suppose many of the riders do see each other repeatedly. They take the same bus at the same time every day to go to work or on Fridays to shop for groceries. They are mostly poor or too young or too old to drive.

I thought maybe I wouldn't buy another car. A personal vehicle is convenient, but it is also isolating. When I have to drive on the freeways, I'm always struck by how humorless the other drivers all look, how almost every vehicle contains only the driver.

Maybe that's the key. Cars are for drivers. Buses are for passengers. Buses are earth friendly, but they are also people friendly. Being on that bus made me feel more like a citizen of Albuquerque.

Sharice knew I was in a cast and had agreed to come to my house for our dinner date. So I had to prepare the meal.

When I reached downtown, I switched from the 54 bus to the 8 and rode to the La Montañita Co-op on Menaul where I bought two fresh trout.

I had to wait an hour in the hot sun for the next number 8 going back west. I hadn't replaced the disappeared hat, and I began to worry about my already abused skin.

And to reassess the idea of depending on buses to get around Albuquerque.

I didn't have to worry about the trout because the nice lady behind the counter had packed them with a little bag of ice.

After I got home and put the trout in the fridge, I crutched down to Miss Gladys and was happy to discover she had some grape leaves left over.

I had slashed an old pair of Levis from cuff to knee on the right leg and worn them every day since getting the cast. Now I faced a dilemma. The split Levis were grungy, and I didn't want to ruin a pair of good trousers. I considered wearing my bathrobe, but quickly dismissed that option.

I threw the split Levis in the washer and started cleaning the trout. I had decided to do *truchas en terracota*, a dish from the menu of *Casa Sena* in Santa Fe.

The trout had been gutted but otherwise unprocessed. I washed them and patted them dry. Trout don't need to be scaled for this dish because the skin is ingeniously removed when they are served.

I filled the cavities with fresh basil, a pinch of freshly ground green peppercorns, salt and piñon nuts, making sure the nuts were all shelled. Another chipped tooth would be bad for me but even worse for Sharice in her line of work as a dental assistant and hygienist.

I wrapped the fish in the grape leaves and encased them in clay. I don't know where *Casa Sena* gets their clay, but mine came from the banks of the Rio Puerco and was dug up at night. It's not illegal to dig for clay. But with my reputation, who would believe that was what I was after?

I put the prepared fish into the fridge and removed a bowl of blue corn *posole* that had been soaking overnight. I transferred the *posole* to a large pan and brought it to a low boil in salted water.

Then I hung the Levis out to dry and took a shower. It was even more refreshing than usual. It's so arid in New Mexico that perspiration evaporates as it forms, so we never feel sweaty. But that's how I felt boarding the buses and waiting for one in front of the Co-op. Maybe not being able to move through the air because of the cast was the problem.

By the time I had showered, shaved, brushed and flossed, the Levis were bone dry. Hey, it's the desert. I pressed a stiff crease into them, thinking as I did so of Stella Ramsey, a former paramour who always comes to mind when I touch an iron.

I put my best dress shirt over the Levis, hoping the combo looked somehow chic. I've never been certain exactly what 'chic' means, but it was the word that sprung to mind every time I saw Sharice.

The water in the *posole* had boiled down almost to the desired level. I reduced the heat and added minced garlic, extra virgin olive oil, a handful of chopped fresh Mexican oregano and a cup of roasted green chile.

I placed two champagne flutes and two bottles of Gruet in the freezer, one a *blanc de noirs* and the other a rosé. I have a refrigerator-door magnet in the shape of a tiny Gruet bottle which I purchased at their gift shop. I stuck it to the freezer door to remind me to remove the champagne after it was icy cold and before it froze and popped its cork.

I lowered the lights and lit the candles.

When the doorbell rang, I put the trout in the oven.

She was stunning in a white dress that went all the way up both front and back to a sort of turtle neck but had no sleeves at all. It didn't have much of a skirt either, so her lovely long legs and arms were daringly displayed.

Her short hair was in a loose afro. Her eye shadow and lipstick were violet. I'd never before seen a woman with violet lips, but against her ash grey skin, those lips generated fantasies that arose quicker than I could suppress them.

She gave me a kiss on the cheek and handed me a stalk of yucca blossoms. Their grapefruit and lemony smell was perfect for a desert evening.

She looked around the shop. "What lovely pottery. Did you make these?"

"Some of them."

She approached one of the display cases and picked up a wide low bowl I had fashioned after one from San Ildefonso.

I looked at my reflection in the glass door of the case.

"Examining your sunburn?"

"No, trying to see if I have a violet lip print on my cheek."

She smiled. "Quality lipstick stays put."

I smiled back. "So I guess you could say it's inviolate."

She groaned and held up the bowl. "Can we use this?"

"Sure."

I escorted her through the workshop and back to the dining room.

She ran some water into the bowl then deftly stripped the yucca stem of its flowers so that they floated in the bowl.

Then she saw Geronimo scratching at the door.

"He's so adorable. Can you let him in?"

He's a real chick magnet. I know Tristan says people don't say 'chick' anymore, but that's what he is.

"He can be a bit rambunctious," I warned. I didn't add that it was only around women.

I opened the door and he jumped at her. The two of them quickly became fast friends forever or whatever that new phrase is.

She opted for the *blanc de noirs* and the patio. Geronimo curled up at her feet and eavesdropped on our conversation which didn't last long because the trout bakes quickly.

I excused myself to set the table while she and Geronimo continued to bond.

I added fresh cilantro and a squeeze of lime to the *posole* and placed some on each plate. Then I brought the trout to the table on a serving platter.

*Truchas in terracotta* is delicious to eat and showy to serve. I struck the clay with the back of a spoon. The clay fissured and Sharice gasped.

"Amazing," she said when I lifted the clay, and the grape leaves and trout skin came away with it, leaving the succulent flesh which had cooked in its own steam.

She complimented me on the trout, the *posole* and my outfit. "The worn old Levis with neat creases look cool over your cast."

"I don't have any other pants that will slip over the cast, so the only option other than the Levis was my bathrobe."

She laughed. "Did you consider it?"

"Yes, but I rejected it quickly."

"Whew."

She looked at the bowl on the table with the yucca blossoms. "Did you make this one?"

I nodded.

"Makes beautiful bowls and cooks. Impressive."

"The bowl is a copy. I can't take credit for the design. And the recipe is from *Casa Sena*. I'm just a copycat."

"Remember those bowls you ask me to x-ray a couple of years ago? Were they copies?"

"Yes . . . or no."

"One of those, I imagine."

She had a soft natural smile that showed her perfect teeth. I was trying to think of her as my date, not my dental hygienist, but those teeth were hard to ignore. Indeed, there was nothing about her I could ignore, neither her bright green eyes, her delicate nose nor the trim firm muscles on her thin arms and legs.

I yanked my mind back to the conversation and tried to explain my hesitation about the pots being copies. "The ancient potters from San Roque made a set of pots they considered sacred. Their descendants made other sets just like them. So you could say they were copies. But when potters make a pot that's part of their culture, I don't think of it as copying. The design belongs to them as members of the tribe."

"Why did you want me to x-ray them?"

"I wanted to see if they were from the original set or from one of the newer sets."

Her brow furrowed. "Something like carbon dating? The originals were older so they would x-rayed differently?"

"I don't know if an x-ray can determine age, but it can detect metal. The originals had gold discs embedded in their bases."

"Wow. And were those originals?"

"They were."

"So you broke them and retrieved the gold?"

"No way. In the first place, I'd never break a genuine ancient pot. The original potter would never forgive me."

She smiled again. I was getting hooked on her smiles. "You believe in spirits?"

"I feel a kinship with the ancient potters. Sometimes I even feel their presence. Maybe it's just in my mind, but it seems real."

"And in the second place?"

"Huh?"

"You said in the first place you'd never break a pot."

"Oh, right. In the second place, the pots were worth more than the gold."

"I'd like to see them again. Or have you sold them?"

"I gave them back to the Ma."

"The Ma?"

"That's what the people of San Roque call themselves."

"You gave them back because they were sacred?"

I nodded.

"Can I ask you a personal question?"

I smiled at her. "Yes, I think I can make love even with a cast on."

The way she laughed told me my little joke hadn't offended her. "You're witty, Hubie."

"Shoot. I was trying for sexy."

Her demure look told me there was no prospect of us making love that evening.

Which was fine with me. Call me old-fashioned, but I like to get to know a woman before I jump in bed with her. Of course I couldn't have jumped in bed given my cast. And I have been known to break my get-to-know-them rule. Once, gloriously, with Stella.

That was the second time I'd thought of her that day, and she and Sharice are nothing alike. But when a man has sex on his mind, he's mentally impaired, so it's a wonder I managed even to prepare the food.

"What I wanted to ask is how can you give pots back to the Ma because they are sacred and yet dig up and sell other pots?"

I hesitated because it's a complicated issue.

"Am I out of line?" She asked.

"Not at all. It's just that it's a long boring philosophical answer."

"'Long boring philosophical' is a triple oxymoron."

Beautiful, intelligent and funny. Good teeth, too. I think I was falling in love.

"There was no doubt the pots you x-rayed belonged to the Ma. But when I dig up an ancient pot from a site abandoned a thousand years ago, there are no modern day people who can claim ownership. I already told you how I feel about the ancient potters. I think they want their work to be appreciated."

"Some people say those pots belong to today's First Nations even if they can't be traced to a specific tribe."

"First Nations, eh?"

She giggled. Her giggle was just as intoxicating as her laugh. "Okay, I'm Canadian. We call them First Nations. You yanks call them Native Americans."

"And all the ones I know call themselves Indians. But that sort of makes my point about labels and ethnicity. You're Canadian, but your parents were from Jamaica. Your distant ancestors were from Africa. So do you have a tie to the artwork of Africa, Jamaica or Canada?"

"I've never thought about it."

"My answer would be all three. And all other artwork everywhere. Artifacts are human before they are Native American, Chinese, European or whatever."

I resisted the temptation to drag out one of my Schuze' Anthropological Premises. The evening was progressing too well to be spoiled.

The conversation returned to small talk over dessert which was New Mexican green chile caramel truffles from Cocopotamus, an artisanal chocolate maker here in Albuquerque.

Between her second and third pieces of the chocolate, Sharice said candy is not recommended by those in the dental profession.

I offered to walk her to her car, but she said to the door would be fine. And it did turn out to be a fine place indeed.

She turned in the doorway and asked, "How is the chipped tooth?"

"Fine."

Moonlight glinted off her green eyes. "I think I need to check it." She stepped against me. "Closely."

When the passionate kiss ended, I said, "I could take off the cast."

She laughed and departed.

# 14

I was so smitten by Sharice that I forgot all about the rosé in the freezer.

Luckily, I saw the magnet on the door before turning out the lights. I removed the bottle and was happy to see it had not yet frozen. I was tempted to open it and have a few more pieces of chocolate. Then I remembered my desire to drink less and lose a few pounds. I stuck the rosé in the fridge and tried to forget it was there.

Which was easy to do because thoughts of Sharice filled my head.

The dreams that followed were even better than the thoughts because my censor was off duty.

On Sunday mornings, I normally eat a breakfast so large that it tides me over for the rest of the day. But I was trying to diet. So while I was at the co-op, I'd bought a bottle of Hollywood Diet Juice made from fruit juices, extracts of green tea, biloba and the mandatory preservatives and stabilizers.

I can understand the last two ingredients. Who wants to drink something that's unpreserved and unstable?

All I know about biloba is it sounds like the guy who discovered the Pacific Ocean.

Which must have come as a surprise to the millions of native people who were already living on its shores.

I'm usually suspicious of anything from Hollywood, but I know this stuff has to work. You drink it instead of meals and you lose weight. Duh.

Martin Seepu showed up around three with one of his uncle's pots. My relationship with Martin began when I volunteered for a program run by the University that matched college students with adolescents on the reservations. Sort of a big-brother program for Indian kids.

Our initial meeting was awkward. I suggested things we could do together. He was so unresponsive, I thought maybe he was deaf. Finally, I asked him what he wanted me to do.

He shrugged. Looking down at the ground, he said, "Teach me something."

"What would you like me to teach you?"

"What you know best."

"What I know best is math." I was majoring in it as an undergraduate. I expected that would curtail his desire for me to teach him something, but he just said, "Okay."

So I taught him math. He said very little but learned quickly. I felt awkward because I did all the talking. Eventually, I asked him to teach me something. It was the only way I could think of to make our relationship more balanced. I was too naïve to realize the cultural gulf between us.

I asked him what he knew best, and he said it was how to draw horses. I knew less about drawing than he had known about math. But I started learning and liked it. It was the first time I'd ever attempted anything artistic. And it was good for him because he had to talk to teach. Not much in the beginning, but he eventually came out of his shell.

One reason why so many students dislike abstract math is they don't see any purpose for it. Arithmetic is all you need in life. Why waste time on algebra? But most Indians don't think that way. Because they are marginalized in our economic system, the question of the utility of knowledge is not so important for them.

It is a morally satisfying irony that Martin, who dropped out of school at thirteen, is more intellectual than college students studying to become engineers or doctors. They learn to practice a profession. He learns because he believes it is better to know than not to know.

"I'll chance some of your coffee," he said.

"I've got some Gruet rosé in the fridge."

"Just coffee."

"If you don't drink the Gruet, I'm afraid I will."

"Even if I drink it, you just open another one."

He knows me well.

I poured us both a cup of coffee. He took a sip and asked what happened to my ankle. I gave him an abbreviated version of my cliff dwelling adventure.

When I finished, he said, deadpan, "So you've become a grave robber."

"It wasn't a grave." I had summarized for Martin all the options Susannah and I had kicked around on that topic.

He nodded. "I agree a murderer wouldn't haul his victim down there to bury him, but there's another option."

I thought about it for about the hundredth time, but no new explanations came to me.

"So what is this other possibility?"

"You taught me math isn't about numbers. It's about reasoning. Take your one fact and combine it with two assumptions. The fact is there's a guy buried there. The first assumption is he was murdered. The—"

"That's a stretch."

"That's why it's an assumption. The second assumption is that a murderer wouldn't haul a body down there. So what follows by reason?"

I did abandon math for accounting, but I didn't forget simple reasoning. "The murderer was already down there."

He nodded.

"Okay," I admitted, "the logic is flawless. But it depends on two premises. The first is that two people were down there together. The second is that one them decided to kill the other one. Those both seem highly improbable."

"Maybe not so improbable. Maybe they were a couple of pot hunters. They got in an argument about splitting the loot, and one killed the other."

The more I thought about it, the more it made some sense. And the more uncomfortable I felt. Not about whether the dead guy was murdered, but about myself.

I like to compare myself to Howard Carter who found King Tut or to the fictional Indiana Jones. I see treasure hunters as dashing romantic figures.

But there is a seamy side to my profession. It's estimated that illegally gathered artifacts in the United States constitute a billion dollar black market. The epicenter of that illicit industry is the Four Corners, the place where Arizona, Utah, Colorado and New Mexico meet. Archaeologists estimate there are four-hundred-thousand abandoned settlements and two million graves in that area.

The diggers there are not romantic figures. They are often more like gangsters. They use backhoes. They damage more artifacts than they sell. And they carry guns.

That's a far cry from me digging with my hands under a desert moon and treating my finds with care and affection. But as the saying goes, if you lie down with dogs, you'll get up with fleas. I was beginning to fear I might be part of the problem.

Martin held up the pot he'd brought. "You can get this one without digging in a grave."

His uncle is a gifted potter. This was one of his smaller pots, about six inches high with a circumference the size of a grapefruit. The colors were sienna and pomegranate, and the design was traditional to their pueblo.

"Unfortunately, I don't have the money to buy it."

"You want it on consignment?"

"Sure. How much does he want for it?"

"He's hoping for a thousand."

"Okay. Maybe it will attract some customers. I could use some."

# 15

It took me fifteen minutes to make what is normally a three minute walk from my shop, through the plaza and over to *Dos Hermanas*, primarily because I had to take two rest stops.

I leaned the crutches against our table at *Dos Hermanas* and said, "I'm sweating like a pig."

"Pigs don't sweat, Hubie. That's why they have to wallow in mud to stay cool."

"You raise sheep and cattle, not pigs."

"But I know about pigs. I was an ag major for a while."

"Okay, I'm sweating like a dog."

"Dog's don't sweat—they pant."

I threw up my hands. "Then I'm sweating like a human. But even we humans don't sweat this much in the desert. I think it must be the crutches."

After we ordered, I told her how stunning Sharice looked in her shoulderless dress. She commented that most men don't notice how a woman is dressed.

"It wasn't so much the dress I noticed as what it revealed."

"So she has a good figure?"

"Not in the traditional sense. She's thin and sort of flat-chested with long limbs."

"*Gamine.*"

"I don't know what that means," I said.

"I learned it in art history. It's a waifish girl, thin but somehow appealing." She pulled her cell phone from her purse, punched a few keys and showed me an oil painting on the screen. "This is *Le Nu Gris* by Pierre Bonnard. His nudes are often described as gamine. Is this what Sharice looks like?"

"Even thinner," I said. "And her skin is a lot darker."

"I think I could have guessed the skin color part, Hubert, since you told me she's black."

"Sharice also had on clothes, sort of."

"Skimpy dress, huh?"

"It had almost enough material to make a pillow case, but somehow it didn't seem skimpy. It was like a good meeting, short enough to—"

She held up a palm. "I know, short enough to be interesting but long enough to cover the subject." She shook her head. "Saying things like that dates you, Hubie."

I thought it was funny, but maybe she's right.

"She was angelic in that white dress with a stem of yucca blossoms in her hand."

"She brought you a stem of yucca blossoms? That is so romantic. What happened next?"

The only thing Susannah likes better than a mystery is a romance.

"I wowed her with my *savoir faire.*"

"A side of you I don't know? Come on, Hubie—details."

"For starters, I cleaned and pressed these Levis."

"A ripped pair of old Levis you've worn every day for two weeks hardly qualifies as *savoir faire*."

"You should have seen them with that razor-edged pleat I ironed in. And contrasting them with my favorite dress shirt was chic."

"I've never understood what that means."

"Me neither. But Sharice said the Levis looked cool over my cast. When I removed the clay from the *truchas en terracotta*, she said, 'Makes beautiful bowls and cooks'. So I figure a guy who can make old Levis seem chic, throw a beautiful bowl and serve a fancy meal must have *savoir faire*."

"Sheesh. Did you tell her you're a pot thief?"

"She already knew that. But we did talk about it. I think she liked the fact that I returned the sacred pots to the Ma, but she wondered how that fits in with keeping other pots I dig up."

"I hope you didn't drag out any of your Anthropological Theses."

"Would a guy with *savoir faire* do that?"

"So she's okay with what you do."

I took a sip of my margarita. For some reason, the ones *Dos Hermanas* makes on Mondays seem to be the best. "She's fine with it. I'm not sure I am. I've been bouncing between happy and sad. I would fret about the dead guy. Then I'd think about my upcoming date with Sharice and be happy. It was fun being with Tristan who has to drive me everywhere. Then I got depressed about all the criminal types who are also pot hunters."

"Hmm. Mood swings and a lot of sweating. Must be menopause," she said, putting the stress on 'men'.

"And you think my good meeting joke is bad?"

We both chuckled. The past few days had been out of character for me. I'm almost always happy, especially when I'm with Susannah. Even our corny jokes make me laugh.

"Still worried about the dead guy you desecrated?"

I laughed some more. "Thanks for putting it so delicately. Martin came by yesterday. Something he said got me to thinking about the black market in antiquities, and I began to feel dirty."

"What was it he said?"

"He came up with a new theory about the body above the Rio Doloroso."

She straightened in her chair, and her big eyes grew even larger.

"He said it's possible a pair of pot hunters were there. They got into an argument over splitting the loot, and one of them killed his partner."

"That's brilliant. You had a good point, Hubie, that a murderer wouldn't carry his victim's body along a narrow dangerous path just to bury it in an old cliff dwelling. But Martin's explanation blows your point right out of the water."

"No it doesn't. It explains how a murderer could *bury* the guy there without having to *carry* him down there. But it does so by substituting one wacky story for another. Two guys in the middle of pillaging a cliff dwelling breaking into a fatal argument is just as unlikely as a murderer carrying his victim's body down there."

"No it isn't. Most pot hunters are not as genteel as you. I can see them getting into a fight."

So now I was back to the evils of the antiquities trade and the ethics of my being involved in it.

"That's what I meant about me not being comfortable with what I do."

I told her about the thugs who carry guns and work with crews, construction equipment and large vans to carry away the loot.

"Guns? They would shoot a park ranger?"

"I wouldn't doubt it. But the primary reason they carry guns is to fend off other looters. And here's what's really sick. The thing they most like to find is an infant's grave."

"Oh, ick. Why?"

"Because infants were buried with cradle boards, blankets and amulets, all of which bring big bucks from collectors."

"That is so sick. I hope the amulets work and the people who dig up babies and the people who buy from them find tarantulas in their sheets."

"A lot of people believe disturbing graves puts an evil spell on you," I said, "like the curse of King Tut's tomb."

"I saw that film. It was great. Casper Van Dien is hot."

"I meant the real curse."

"There really was a curse on Tut's tomb?"

"Maybe. Right after the tomb was opened, the guy who financed the expedition, Lord Carnarvon, died."

"People die all the time, Hubie."

"From a mosquito bite?"

"He really died of a mosquito bite?"

"Yep. And there was an inscription on Tut's tomb saying that anyone who disturbed it would be visited by 'winged death' which could be a mosquito."

"Wow."

"And his dog dropped dead the same night."

"The mosquito had a dog?"

"No, Lord Carnarvon had the dog. Of course his death and his dog's death could be coincidences," I said and pointed at her.

She took the cue and said, "There are no coincidences." Then she asked if I believe in curses.

"Sort of. I like to think that evil comes back on those who do it."

"But you don't think digging up old pots will curse you?"

"I think the potters want me to find their work. But lately I've been wondering whether my actions are somehow part of the ugly side of the antiquities trade."

She was looking right into my eyes. "I love that you question your own ethics. That alone shows you're not the sort to do anything wrong. You can't compare yourself with those criminals."

"I'm a criminal, too, Susannah."

"Well, technically. But what you do can't really be called looting. You don't destroy sites. You're careful about how you dig. You revere what you find. You don't dig on reservations. You don't dig in graves . . ."

We stared at each other. Then we broke out laughing.

When we finally stopped, she said, "Hey, one little accident can be overlooked." Then she grew serious again. "So what are you going to do?"

I took a deep breath.

My resolve was weak. Telling her would reinforce my decision to go back. I was satisfied with that decision ethically, but I was still struggling with it emotionally. I didn't want to do it.

But I had to.

"I'm going back to the cliff dwelling to examine that hand. If it's an ancient hand, I'm going to leave something to atone for disturbing the site and then let the body rest in peace. If it's the hand of a contemporary, I'm going to report it to the police."

She smiled. "See, you are a good person. I knew you'd do the right thing. When will you go?"

"In a month or so."

"You are such a procrastinator."

"No I'm not. I'm waiting a few more years before becoming a procrastinator."

"Be serious. Why not go now?"

I pointed down to my cast.

"Oh," she said.

"Koehler said I should wear the cast for about six weeks. It's been about two already. That's why I said a month."

Her wheels were turning. "I think you should go now."

"I can't maneuver that rugged path with a cast."

"I know that. I also know you don't want to do it even without a cast. So why not go down the way you did the first time?"

"The Bronco was stolen, remember?"

"My dad and both brothers have pick-ups with winches. I can borrow one."

"Thanks, but that won't work. I can't drive."

She smiled. "But I can."

# 16

Which is why the next morning found us on our way to Willard, forty miles due southeast from Albuquerque as the crow flies.

But even a crow would have trouble getting there directly. It would need to rise above 10,000 feet to clear the Manzano Mountains.

There's no road over the Manzanos, so you have to go around them on the north or the south. We decided to go one way and return by the other.

A coin flip had us headed south to Belen in Susannah's 1995 Ford Crown Victoria. It was just past eleven in the morning and already in the nineties. The Crown Vic's electric windows died years ago and are permanently stuck in the open position. It's not a problem because it rarely rains here, and no one is going to steal the thing. In fact, having the windows open is an asset since the air conditioning doesn't work.

But a dry wind coming at you at seventy miles an hour is hardly cooling. And it wasn't helping the parchment that was on my face where my skin used to be. It felt like a rebar could easily poke a hole in it.

We made Belen in thirty minutes. Susannah insisted we stop at Harla May's Fat Boy Grill. I was skeptical until I saw that the eatery is located in an abandoned movie theater. At that point I abandoned skepticism in favor of defiance.

But Susannah is hard to resist, especially when she has the wheel. I knew we were in trouble when I spotted their slogan, "We relish your buns." I am not making this up.

Susannah ordered a Holley's Hawaiian burger with pineapple and green chile, a combination I couldn't get my mind around.

And didn't want to get my mouth around.

I went for the Flame Thrower, a burger with hot green chile from the village of Jarales just down the road and grown by the Padilla family.

The server must have taken us for tourists because she asked me if I liked hot food.

I smiled at her and said, "Would I order something called a Flame Thrower if I didn't?"

The burger lived up to its name. My failure to finish it was not owing to its heat. It was because its full pound of ground beef didn't fit my diet plan.

I put down the unfinished half of the burger and said, "I think there's a flaw in Martin's two pot hunters scenario."

Susannah had a mouthful of Hawaiian burger and signaled with her eyebrows for me to continue.

"I can buy two guys working as a team. I can even buy them getting into a fight that leads one of them to kill the other. What I don't buy is the murderer hanging around to dig a two-foot-deep grave."

I waited for her to finish chewing, but I already knew from the expression on her face that she had a rebuttal.

"That's what murderers do. Disposing of the body is one of the major components of a murder mystery."

"This is real life, Susannah."

"I know, but murder mysteries have to be true to life or no one would read them."

"Then how do you explain science fiction?"

"That's also true to life."

"Huh?"

"The science may be fiction, but the people aren't. Take *Star Wars*. The love story between Luke Skywalker and Princess Leia was just like true romance."

"Except for the fact that they were twins."

"They weren't twins in *Star Wars*. That happened later in one of the sequels."

I opened my mouth but closed it again when I realized no good could come from pursuing that line of reasoning.

Then I opened it again and asked, "Why waste all that time and effort digging a grave? Why not just toss the body over the ledge?"

"Someone might find it."

The conversation had a familiar ring to it. "So what? The corpse isn't going to sit up and announce who killed it."

"But if the person who finds the body—unlike someone I won't mention—reports it to the police right away, at least they'll know the guy is dead."

"The guy is going to be dead for a long time, Suze. What difference does it make how soon it's reported?"

"If it's reported early, the CSI guys might be able to find clues that will identify the murderer."

"CSI?"

"Crime scene investigation."

"Oh, right. Well, the clues are just like the dead guy—they aren't going anywhere either."

"They might. Buzzards could carry some away. Ants could—"

"Stop. I just ate half a pound of meat and hot chiles. I don't want to hear this."

I took a gulp of water and said, "From what you said, burying the guy is more likely to preserve clues than is throwing him into the gorge."

"Well, we won't know why he buried him until the police catch him."

"I don't think there's a him to catch."

"You think the murderer was a woman?"

I chuckled. "No, I don't think there *is* a murderer. I think the dead guy died of natural causes a thousand years ago."

"Well, Hubie, that's what you're going to find out when I winch you down that cliff."

My stomach turned.

# 17

New Mexico highway 6 southeast out of Belen crosses dry desolate country, but I love it because it follows along the railroad route called the Belen cutoff, a major part of railroad lore.

The cutoff was built by the Atchison, Topeka and Santa Fe Railway in 1908 to bypass the steep grades of Raton Pass. As many as 150 trains a day roll past the southern end of the Manzano Mountains. That's one about every ten minutes.

Unfortunately, not a single one of them is a passenger train.

New Mexico now has its own passenger train, the sparkling Railrunner that shuttles passengers to points between Santa Fe and Belen, but Belen is the end of the line. You can't take the Belen cutoff around the south end of the Manzanos and on to the rest of the country.

Since losing the Bronco, I'd been thinking about public transportation. Susannah and I were cruising along NM 6 consuming a dollar's worth of gasoline every four miles. A current ad for a train company claims they can move a ton of freight five hundred miles on a single gallon of fuel. I did the math in my head. They could move Susannah and me from Belen to Willard for thirteen cents!

Okay, I know it's not that simple. They'd have to have conductors and ticket takers and other things associated with passengers. But how expensive can it be? The Crown Vic was going to guzzle sixteen dollars worth of gasoline to get us from Belen to Willard. Sixteen dollars versus thirteen cents.

As we neared Willard my thoughts moved from transportation to the matter at hand. "What are we going to say if your family asks why we're borrowing a truck?"

"Tell them we need a winch."

"What if they ask why?"

"Just tell them your Bronco was stolen."

I shook my head. "What I'm trying to find out is how we avoid telling them what we're going to do."

"Why would we avoid telling them?"

"You don't think they might find it just a tad unusual that you're going to lower me into a cliff dwelling so I can partially unearth a corpse and examine its hand?"

"Not really. They know you're a pot hunter."

We rode along in silence while I thought about how I felt about the entire Inchaustigui clan knowing about my unearthing a corpse.

I reached no conclusion on that topic, but something else occurred to me.

"There's also the fact that telling them will make them accessories to a crime."

"All they're doing is lending us a truck."

"And if they know we're going to use it to commit a crime, then they're accessories. And remember that ARPA allows any vehicle used in illegal digging to be confiscated."

"But you won't be digging for pots. You'll be digging to see if there's something to report to the police. You're being a good citizen."

"Actually—"

"You *are* going to dig for pots?"

"Well, I figured as long as I was going down there anyway . . ."

"What about your rule of never digging in a grave?"

"We already had this discussion. You said it wouldn't be grave robbing to dig *close* to a grave. I know where the body is because I put that stone on it. And like you said, there surely aren't any other bodies there. So I figured I'd check the hand then dig around elsewhere to see what I find."

"Maybe you should dig for the pots first. Knowing how squeamish you are, you probably wouldn't be able to search for pots after examining the hand."

She was right.

I watched the trains.

We didn't go all the way to Willard. We turned off the highway six miles short of the village onto a dirt road to Broncho. I don't know if the place was named after a type of horse by someone who couldn't spell or by someone who thought the dry air was good for the lungs. I didn't see any signs of human habitation, so I'm not even sure there *is* a place, but it is on the topo maps. And as you already know, I know every place name in the State from studying those maps for so many years.

After five miles, we arrived at the Inchaustigui home, a two-story house of local fieldstone surrounded by western catalpas. A big reddish dog with a pointed snout and floppy ears rocketed off the front porch and ran circles around Susannah as we approached the house.

Susannah's mom greeted us at the door. I've met Susannah's family briefly a few times when they visited her in Albuquerque, but I got a big hug like a member of the family.

"It's nice to see you again, Mrs. Inchaustigui."

"Mrs. Inchaustigui is my mother-in-law. Call me Hilary, Hubie."

She led us to the kitchen and gave us a choice of water or coffee. I chose a cooling glass of water.

Susannah's father, Gus, was at a ranchers meeting in Las Cruces. The two sons were out somewhere mending fences or fending off coyotes. Hilary called them on a cell phone.

"You can use Matt's truck or Mark's truck. We also have a ranch truck with a winch. What are you planning to do with it?"

Susannah said, "I'm going to lower Hubie into a cliff dwelling so he can dig up a dead guy he found there."

So much for not telling them what we planned to do.

Hilary seemed unfazed by our plan. "Is it a mummy?" she asked me.

"That's what I want to find out."

"He was digging for pots," Susannah chimed in, "and found a body. Actually, all he found was a hand." She looked at me. "It must have been attached to a body, right?"

"I assume so," I said. Susannah and her mom were talking as if this were a normal conversation, so I just went along for the ride.

She turned back to her mom. "So Hubie and I have been debating whether the body is a mummy or some modern person who might have been killed."

Hilary looked at me with a smile exactly like her daughter's. "I'm sure Susannah is the one who thinks it's a murder victim."

"Moms know everything," I said.

"Do you have a wager riding on it?"

I started to answer, but Susannah jumped in. "No, but I think that's a great idea. What should we wager, Hubie?"

"Er . . ."

"Don't say anything that will embarrass your old-fashioned mom," said Hillary.

I had no idea what she meant by that, but I didn't like the sound of it.

"We can talk about it on the way back," I said.

Matt and Mark arrived, and I braced for two crushing hand-shakes. The two brothers are in their early twenties and look like the football players they were.

The four of them spent the next hour in a family chat I enjoyed listening to. It was good to see Susannah with her brothers and her mom who called her Sorne.

Before we left, the boys insisted I take a tour of the place with them. I know they're proud of the place and probably like showing it off, but I assumed the real motive was to give Susannah and her Mom some time alone with each other.

As we rode along, they pointed out a peak off to the east. They were impressed I identified it as Jumanes Knob. They didn't know I've been studying New Mexico topological maps for over twenty years.

And that I have a pot in my shop that came from just below Jumanes Knob. The pot is from the Tompiro people who died out in the 1600s and is decorated with their distinctive asymmetrical cross-hatched shapes. I have it priced at thirty thousand because few complete Tompiro pots have ever been found. Frankly, they are unattractive compared to pueblo pottery from the same period, which is why it hasn't sold. I'm waiting for a customer who appreciates the rarity of the pot.

It was a desolate place back when I found that pot, so searching there was safe. Now there's a wind farm on the mesa with a dozen employees who might spot me if I were digging at the base of the slope.

Looking at those giant turbines made me think about the strange collection of assets that have attracted humans to this area over the last thousand years or so. The Tompiro came here because of the dry lake beds. They harvested the salt and traded it with both the plains Indians to their east and the pueblo peoples to their west. After the arrival of the Spanish, families settled here to farm the rich soil. Torrance County eventually became the 'Pinto Bean Capital of the World' with almost 800 carloads shipped out from the railhead at Mountainair during peak production. A decade-long drought ended farming and led to ranching. Salt, soil, and grass are now giving way to a new asset—wind.

We stopped at a stock tank fed by an old-fashioned windmill. Looking past that venerable Aeromotor up to the giant turbines on the mesa filled me with a sense of passage. I wondered if a generation from now, city kids passing through on vacation would see those turbines as quaint indicators of rural life just as we now regard the old windmills.

It was then I discovered I was wrong about the ulterior motive of the tour. It was not to get Susannah and her mother alone together.

It was to get me and the brothers alone together.

We were standing by the windmill when Matt said to me, "You seem like a nice guy, Hubie."

There was no edge to his voice and no scowl on his face, but somehow I felt uncomfortable.

"Thanks," I said, "You two also seem like good guys. Of course that's what I would expect based on knowing Susannah."

"She's very special to us," said Mark.

"I'm sure she is."

They looked at each other. Some silent brother communication passed between them by means of which it was decided that Matt would speak.

He looked me in the eyes. "What are your intentions regarding Susannah?"

"Completely honorable," I said reflexively.

They both patted me on the back, and we got back in the truck.

I realized immediately I had misled them. Friendship is an honorable thing, but they probably didn't take my answer to mean that. I couldn't think of any way to explain things that didn't seem terribly awkward, so I just let it pass. If they didn't know their sister and I are just friends, they would figure it out soon enough or she would tell them.

It would all work out with a minimum of embarrassment.

# 18

We got closer to Willard on the way back than we did coming in, but still missed it, turning north on State Highway 41 less than a mile from town.

If we hadn't already eaten in Belen, I would have argued for going the extra mile into Willard for a stop at the Willard Cantina & Café, a mom and pop place run by Alex and Lisa Garcia. They serve hamburgers with green chile described on their sign as 'chile with attitude'. Delicious. You can smell it from the parking lot.

Highway 41 reaches Interstate 40 with geometric simplicity—a straight line thirty miles long. It seems boring, but once you enter I 40 and start line-dancing with the eighteen wheelers, you long for that empty two-lane road.

Susannah said, "So what should we wager on whether the dead guy is ancient or modern?"

"Before we decide that, maybe you can tell me what your mom

meant when she said we shouldn't say anything that will embarrass your old-fashioned mom."

"Well, she is old-fashioned, and people make crazy wagers these days. I guess she didn't want to know about it if one of us had to sky dive or run naked across the Old Town Plaza."

I wasn't sure that was what her mother had meant, but she's Susannah's mom, so I didn't argue the point.

"I hope you have a saner wager in mind, because I'm not doing either of those things."

She thought about it for a minute. "I've got a great one. We'll wager my car. If I lose, I have to keep it. If you lose, you have to take it."

"You're going to lose, so what are you going to do about transportation? I can tell you the buses are a challenge."

"I'm not going to lose. But if I do, it will be the perfect excuse to buy another car."

"You already have a perfect excuse. It's back at the ranch waiting for you to reclaim it when you return this truck."

"I can't buy another car while my current one is still working. That would be wasteful. But if I lose it to you in a bet, then I'd be forced to buy another car and wouldn't feel guilty about it."

Instead of commenting on her logic, I said, "In this case you're not going to lose it to me. You're going to win it to me."

After we laughed at that and agreed to the wager, I asked her if 'Sorne' was a nickname.

"Nope. That's my real name, given to me by my Grandfather."

"Gutxiarkaitz."

"Wow. You remember my grandfather's name."

"It's hard to forget. And even harder to pronounce."

"You were close."

"Thanks. So where did 'Susannah' come in?"

"My parents didn't want to disappoint my grandfather by not accepting the Basque name he gave me, but they also wanted me to have what they called 'an American name'. 'Susannah' starts with the same letter and they think it has a western ring to it."

"Your grandfather named your father Gus. That's not a Basque name, is it?"

"No, and it's not his real name either. His name is Eguzki. 'Gus' is his American name, chosen because it sounds like his real name."

"Let me guess—your mom is not really named Hilary."

"Good guess. Her name is Hilargi."

"Is that the Basque equivalent of Hilary?"

"There is no Basque equivalent of Hilary. There is no Basque equivalent of anything. It's not an Indo-European language, remember? There are no cognates."

"Does Hilargi have a meaning?"

"It means 'moon'."

"And 'Eguski'?"

She smiled. "It means 'sun'. My mom always says she knew they were meant for each other when she found out what his name means."

"What are Matt's and Mark's real names?"

"Matt and Mark."

"They don't have Basque names?"

"No. My grandfather passed away before they were born. My parents didn't bother with a Basque name. My mom can't even speak it."

"And 'Sorne'?"

"It means 'conception'."

"So if you were Hispanic, your name would be *Concepcion*."

She shook her head. "I don't think so. *Concepcion* refers to the Immaculate Conception. 'Sorne' means conception in the everyday sense. My parents were married seven years before I was born. My grandfather was so happy when he learned his daughter-in-law was pregnant that he named me for the event that caused it."

As we cruised down I 40, I debated whether to mention my conversation with her brothers.

The nays won the debate.

# 19

Susannah dropped me off around six.

We didn't have time for *Dos Hermanas* because the fall semester had started, and she had the first meeting of her Baroque Art class at 6:30.

As she hates to hear me say about her rule never to miss class, if it's not Baroque, don't fix it.

I called Tristan and asked him to drop by in the morning with the topo maps I needed.

I hobbled over to the fridge. The only things in there were the Gruet rosé, some limp cilantro, a white onion and what might have once been a fruit of some type.

"Another dieting opportunity at hand," I said out loud.

My stomach rumbled in reply.

I decided to read. The only book I had was *Ben-Hur*, so I gave it another try. The portion I read described a meal of "wine in small gurglets of skin" and dried mutton. This was prefaced by an explanation of how the character cleaned his camel's nose.

I don't like wine unless it has bubbles. I suspect I would like it even less in a gurglet of skin, whatever that is.

I closed *Ben-Hur* and opened the phone book to the restaurant section to see what I could have delivered. Surely I could do better than dried mutton.

I rarely phone out for meals because I don't eat pizza or Chinese food. I was hoping there might be another choice. I saw a listing for a place called Lettuce Cater and was just starting to dial when Miss Gladys appeared at my door with one of her canvas bags trimmed in checked gingham, a sight for sore eyes and an empty stomach.

In keeping with her new international theme, it was an Irish casserole, although I suspect no one in Dublin has ever tasted anything like it.

"This one came from Marsha Garcia."

"Marsha Garcia was Irish?"

"Heavens no. She was a deep-roots Texan. Her great, great, great grandfather was Gregorio Esparza, one of the six *Tejanos* who died alongside Crockett and Bowie in the Alamo. She got the inspiration from a corned beef sandwich she ate on St. Patrick's Day at a restaurant in San Antonio. They served it with green beer, but I don't have any of that."

"Thanks."

Her eyes twinkled. "For the casserole or for not having any green beer."

"Both."

"This one practically put itself together. You don't even have to measure. You start by tearing pumpernickel bread into pieces and putting them into a buttered casserole dish. You can get rid of old bread this way because dried bread absorbs the flavors better. You cover the bread with diced corned beef then a jar of sauerkraut then a bag of shredded Swiss cheese. Next you mix a carton of eggs, a jar of ranch dressing and a can of Campbell's Cream of Celery Soup and pour the mixture over everything. You can bake it right then if you want to, but it's even better if you let it sit in the refrigerator overnight. That way the eggs, dressing and soup really work their way into the bread."

After being around Miss Gladys all these years, I have gotten used to having terms like 'can', 'bag', 'jar' and 'carton' used as recipe amounts.

She was ladling the stuff onto a plate as she spoke. It looked like a corned beef sandwich run through a blender.

"Where do you get the corned beef?"

"I buy it from the deli section of Smith's."

I breathed a sigh of relief that it wasn't from a can, took a bite and wished she had brought the dolmades casserole instead.

The word 'pumpernickel' sounds like a character from a Wagnerian opera, and the taste lasts almost as long.

"What do you think of it?" she asked.

"Miss Gladys, in all the years you've been letting me sample your casseroles, I've never tasted one like this."

"I just knew you would like it."

I took another very small bite.

She canted her head and said, "Did you have a dinner guest Saturday night?"

"I did."

"I thought so. I saw an African-American girl go into your shop Saturday night with a stem of yucca blossoms. Our society has changed, hasn't it?"

"Yes it has. When I was growing up, girls never brought flowers to boys."

She colored slightly. "I was referring to your date being African-American."

"She's not African-American."

"I could have sworn—"

"She's Canadian."

"Oh," she said, slightly confused. "Well, she is very pretty."

"She is."

"Have you known her long?"

"I've known her for three or four years. She works for my dentist as an assistant and a hygienist. Saturday was our first date, but it won't be our last."

"You've asked her out again?"

"She asked me. Women not only bring flowers these days, they also invite men on dates. I'm having dinner at her house on Saturday."

# 20

Even though I had brushed, flossed and gargled with minty mouthwash before retiring, I woke up the next morning with the taste of pumpernickel in my mouth.

I repeated those oral hygiene procedures in the morning, but a faint taste of pumpernickel seemed to linger.

Tristan arrived with the maps I'd requested and breakfast burritos from Casa de Benavidez up on 4th street. They were stuffed with egg, potatoes, red chile and *carne adovada*. One whiff of those burritos and dieting seemed like the worst idea since that product for bald guys called Hair in a Can.

I suspect Sharice would disapprove of my not brushing again after breakfast, but I figured leaving the red chile and *carne adovada* juices in my mouth all day was the only way to rid it of the pumpernickel taste.

"Since you can't drive, I thought I better bring you some nourishment."

"You're a life saver. I don't have any food in the house except for some leftover Irish casserole."

"From Miss Gladys, no doubt. I bet it has corned beef. I like corned beef."

"I don't. But the worst part is the pumpernickel."

"What soup is in it?"

"Cream of celery."

"That doesn't make much sense."

"The entire casserole makes no sense. It has ranch dressing."

"I like that, too."

"Well, at least I'm having a great breakfast thanks to you."

"You've got to get a car."

"I can't afford a car right now. Besides, I may get one free."

"How so?"

"Susannah and I have a wager going. If I lose, I get her car."

"And if you win?"

"Then she has to keep it."

He laughed and asked me what the wager was.

"I used the remote you rigged up for my winch to lower myself into a cliff dwelling to look for pots."

"I figured you wanted it for something like that."

"I didn't find any pots. What I found was a human hand. I assume it was connected to an entire human body, but I can't be sure of that because I immediately covered it back up."

He frowned. "Cliff dwellers didn't bury their dead where they lived."

"That's why I'm going back. Susannah thinks the body is a modern person. I think it's an ancient person. I'm going to unearth the hand again to see which it is. That's what the wager is."

He stared at me in disbelief. "You're going to dig up the body again just to settle a bet?"

"No, no. You know how I feel about digging in graves. I'm not going back to settle a wager. I'm going back because if it's a modern person, I need to report it to the police."

"Why not just report it to the police and let them do the digging?"

That was my original plan. Now I was trying to remember why I had changed it.

Tristan saved me the effort. "Wait, I know. If you report it, you'll get in trouble for the digging."

"Right. But if it's an ancient mummy, then I won't have to report it, but at least my conscience will be clear."

"And if Susannah is right?"

"Then I'll report it and throw myself on the mercy of the court."

"That's what I thought you'd say. But I have a better idea. You're more squeamish than I am. You're also afraid of heights. And you're handicapped with that cast. I'll go down and check the hand for you."

I love that kid.

"I can't let you do that."

"Sure you can." He gave me one of those big dopey smiles of his. "If it will make you feel better about it, we can call it an exchange. I've saved enough this summer to pay half my tuition. You pay the other half, and I do a chore for you."

"It's not a chore," I said. "And it's illegal. I'll pay half your tuition anyway. How much is it?"

"Thirty two hundred this semester."

"Wasn't it twenty nine last semester?"

"Tuition goes up every semester."

"The university hasn't heard about the recession?"

"Universities are recession-proof. Tuition at public universities across the country has risen more than 65 percent over the past decade while median family income has risen only 5 percent."

I remembered reading a similar statistic about healthcare. At the rate those two are inflating, all our income will eventually go to improving our minds and repairing our bodies. There won't be anything left for groceries or rent.

Or buying pots.

"When I was a student, tuition was five hundred dollars a year."

"Yeah, and gas was a dollar a gallon. Hey, I can get a student loan."

"I don't want you to do that. It's crazy to graduate and have to use most of the income from your first job to pay off loans."

"I'll have to pay you back just like paying back a bank."

"We'll discuss that when the time comes. I'm more flexible than a bank. I'll have the money for you next week."

I didn't know where I would get it.

"When we were at your dentist's office," he said, "you told me you had a date with that hygienist."

"Sharice."

"Yeah, how did it go?"

"Great. She came to my place because it was easier than going out with this cast."

"And who would date a cast anyway?"

"Oh, no. You're beginning to make my kind of jokes. I enjoyed the evening, and I think she did, too. She invited me to her place this coming Saturday."

"Excellent."

I asked him how much the maps cost so I could reimburse him.

"Thirty two cents."

"Funny. How much were they really?"

"I'm not joking. They're free from the U.S. Geological Survey online. The only expense is the paper and ink to print them off. It costs me eight cents a page to print the four adjacent maps you asked for. It would have been more if I printed them in color. You didn't need them in color did you?"

I thought about it then said with a smile, "No, black and white is good."

# 21

Tristan took the Irish casserole. He thanked me for giving it to him, and I thanked him for taking it.

Susannah had to work the lunch shift at *La Placita* so I had a few hours to kill before we departed.

I wanted to read to get my mind off the upcoming task, but I'd had enough of Lew Wallace. *Ben-Hur* and *The Wooing of Malkatoon* were both due back to the library. I had enough time to return the books and check out some new ones.

It wasn't until I stood up that I remembered the pottery on my foot.

Tristan was right. I needed a car.

The bong sounded, and I looked up to see Dolly Madison Aguirre entering my shop.

She wore a broomstick skirt in a red bandana print and a fitted white blouse that showed off her ample breasts. Her dark hair was in a bob, and her skin was as lustrous and smooth as I remembered.

I came out from behind the counter and said "Hi" because a simple greeting seemed the best way to brush aside the unpleasantness of our last meeting.

"Hi, Hubie. What happened to your foot?"

"I sprained my ankle. No big deal. How are you?"

When she opened her mouth to speak, her chin trembled slightly. She closed her mouth, swallowed hard then said, "My father passed away."

"Oh, Dolly," I said and hobbled towards her. We hugged while she continued to sob.

When that passed she moved out of my arms.

"Let's have coffee," I said. "I have some New Mexico Piñon brewed."

"That would be nice."

When the coffee was poured and we were seated at my table, I asked her when her father had died.

"A little over two weeks ago. I knew you would want to know. I called you several times. Then I came by two days in a row both during the day and at night. I guess you were out of town."

I was out of town all right. The first night sleeping in a cliff dwelling with a dog and a coyote and the next night out in the open with the same two companions.

"The funeral was the day after my second visit. Then I came back to tell you about a memorial service at the school, but you were gone then too."

Making a round trip to the Inchaustigui ranch to get a truck in order to go back to the cliff dwelling and dig up the a dead guy when I should have been paying last respects to a man I liked and admired.

I was feeling lower than a gopher in a gulch.

115

"I'm sorry I missed the funeral and the memorial service. And even sorrier I wasn't here for you. I remember how I felt when my father died."

"I still can't believe he's gone. Even though we knew he was dying, it still came as a shock. I guess nothing can prepare you for the reality of it. The finality of it."

I put my hand on the table. She squeezed it.

"Where is he buried? I'd like to at least visit his grave."

A sad smile formed on her face. "He was cremated and his ashes scattered as he directed. You'll like this, Hubie. You remember that grove of trees next to the irrigation ditch where we picnicked?"

I nodded.

"He used to go there to read. His will directed that his ashes be dumped in the irrigation ditch when it was full and flowing. He said . . ." She choked up for a minute. When she continued, she said, "He said he wanted to be absorbed by tree roots and aspirated into the atmosphere as oxygen to help make up for all the carbon dioxide he had put into the air with his long lectures."

We laughed and cried simultaneously.

"He did get wound up when it was a topic he loved," I said.

"And he loved them all," she replied.

We sat in silence for a minute.

"I feel lucky our paths crossed," I said.

"No hard feelings?"

"You're the one who should have hard feelings. I was a typical insensitive male who didn't even bother to ask myself why your behavior had changed a bit."

"Changed a bit? You mean morphed from Dorothy into the Wicked Witch of the West?"

I laughed. "It wasn't that bad. All I remember are the good

times. And if it weren't for you, I never would have reconnected with your father."

There was another long silence.

"What will you do now?" I asked.

"You're going to think I'm still having mood swings and making snap decisions, but I really did think this out even though it's been barely more than two weeks. I'm booked on an around-the-world cruise."

It was such an unexpected announcement that I made no response whatsoever. But my expression must have given me away.

"You think I'm crazy," she said.

"I've always thought you were a bit crazy. That's one of the things I love about you."

"But this is more than just a little crazy, right?"

"You know I don't like to travel, so I'm the worst possible person to make a judgment on a long cruise. And it doesn't matter what I think. If a cruise is what you want, you should do it. I know you loved caring for your father, but it did confine you. I bet you haven't been out of Albuquerque for five years."

"Nine, actually."

"When will you be back?"

She looked down for a moment. "I don't know. I have a flight to San Diego in the morning. We embark in the afternoon. We go to Cabo San Lucas, Puerto Vallarta, Costa Rica and then through the Panama Canal. From there we go to Aruba and Martinique before crossing the Atlantic to the Canary Islands, Casa Blanca and past Gibraltar into the Mediterranean."

"I'm seasick just thinking about it," I said.

"I've forgotten where we go next, but the cruise has an option of staying in any of the ports of call and then catching the next ship a month or so later. When I find a place I really like, I'm going to do that."

"Will you send me a post card?"

"Do you want me to?"

"Sure. I'll never visit any of those exotic places, but I'm still interested in them. And I'd like to know how you're doing."

There was another long silence.

"Are you seeing anyone?" she asked.

"I am."

"Rats. I was hoping we could have a roll in the hay before I left. But maybe it's just as well. A girl could be injured by that cast."

I appreciated the break in the tension.

"Maybe when you get back, I won't be seeing anyone. I don't have a track record of long relationships."

"At least you haven't been divorced three times."

So that was the number. I have to admit I had wondered

"All that proves," I said, "is there are three dopes in the world."

"That's nice of you to say. I felt like such a failure, divorced for the third time and moving back in with my dad. But mom had died, and he needed me. It turned out to be a happy arrangement. He appreciated me more than any of my husbands did, and taking care of him made me feel useful. Then you came along and added romance to my life."

"Gee, I thought it was you adding romance to mine."

She stood up so I did the same. She offered her hand and I took it. We walked to the front door. Actually, she walked and I hobbled using her hand for balance.

We kissed.

"Goodbye, Hubie."

# 22

"You seem kind of down."

Susannah and I were in the truck headed north on I 25. It was their ranch truck, but it still had comforts like air conditioning and useful tools like a winch and a rifle mounted on a window rack in case a coyote got too close to the sheep.

"I am a bit down. Someone came to see me this morning."

"I know. Tristan brought you breakfast."

"After he left. It was Dolly. She wanted to tell me her father died."

"Oh my God. I'm sorry, Hubie."

"He died while I was looting a grave."

"Don't get melodramatic. You weren't looting a grave. You didn't even know it was a grave."

"If I weren't a criminal, if I had an honest profession, I would have been home when she came by to tell me her father died. I could have comforted her, at least gone to the funeral."

"Come on, Hubie. Even if you had a regular job, you could have been away. You might have been making a sales call, attending a training session, whatever. Being a pot thief is not the only job that can cause you to miss a funeral."

I stared out the window.

"Okay, spit it out," she said. "What's the real problem?"

"When she told me her father died, I realized I never loved her."

She glanced at me briefly. "I don't get it."

"I felt for her. I know what it's like when your father dies. But I felt the same for her as I would have felt for anyone who told me she lost her father. There was nothing out of the ordinary, no sense of truly sharing in her loss. It seems to me . . ."

I was groping for the right phrasing.

"Don't over think it. Just say what you're feeling."

"If I truly loved her, her pain would be mine. But it wasn't. I felt for her loss, but I didn't share it. I actually felt worse about Frank than I did about Dolly."

"Well, duh. Frank was the one who died. No wonder you felt worse for him. Dolly can overcome her grief, but Frank can't overcome death."

"I almost proposed to her last fall."

"I remember that. But she was the one who blocked that by telling you she had no interest in trying marriage again."

"Who can blame her? Three strikes and you're out."

"She was married three times?"

I nodded.

"I wondered what the number was," she said.

"After she left, I felt relieved that I didn't ask her to marry me."

"I thought you didn't care about her previous marriages."

"I didn't. Still don't. The reason I felt relieved about not proposing is I realized I didn't love her. I like her a lot. She's a good person. We had fun together. But I wouldn't have wanted to marry her. And that made me feel sad, as if I had misled her or used her."

"You're an obsessive analyzer, you know that, Hubert? She wouldn't have married you even if you had asked, so stop worrying about it. You didn't use her. If anything, she used you, going out with you with no willingness to make a permanent commitment. She even told you she didn't mind if you saw other women."

"Yeah, but I never did that."

She smiled and said, "What about Maria, the *saucier*?"

"Sleeping on someone's love seat is not a date."

"You were headed for her bed before you fell asleep."

Which led us into a rehash of my misadventures in a restaurant in Santa Fe called *Schnitzel* at first then *Chile Schnitzel* in its reincarnation as Austrian/Southwestern fusion. It was fun to look back and joke about it, and it perked me up a little.

It might have perked me up even more had I not been dreading what lay ahead.

We took the relief route around Santa Fe. I think the normal phrase for it would be a bypass, but nothing is normal in Santa Fe.

I brought the conversation back to Dolly. "You remember the picnic Dolly and I had at *Casitas del Bosque*?"

"How could I forget it? It was your second lame stakeout of the neighborhood."

I chose to ignore her comment.

"Geronimo and I were in that little grove of trees by the irrigation ditch. Several people gave us quizzical looks, and it occurred to me that perhaps the area under the trees was part of the communal property of *Casitas del Bosque*. So I decided to check with the closest resident to make sure I wasn't going to be asked to leave by the neighborhood patrol."

"Yeah, I remember. That was Dolly's house. You asked her if it would be okay if the two of you had a picnic under the trees, and she said okay but give her a minute to put her shoes on."

"Right. But what I meant by 'the two of us' was Geronimo and me. She just misunderstood."

"Anyone would have. Who goes on a picnic with a dog? So why are you telling me this again?"

"Because I want to tell you something nice about Frank Aguirre. Dolly told me his will directed that he be cremated and his ashes dumped into the irrigation ditch that flows by that little grove."

She shook her head. "Geez. Most people want something a little more noble or romantic, like having their ashes scattered on a mountain top or in their favorite trout stream. Who would pick an irrigation ditch?"

"Frank Aguirre, that's who. He wanted his ashes dumped in the irrigation ditch so they would be absorbed by tree roots and aspirated into the atmosphere as oxygen to help make up for all the carbon dioxide he had put into the air with his long lectures."

"Are you serious?"

"That's what Dolly told me."

"I think I would have liked him."

# 23

It was past four when we turned off the highway just west of the low water bridge. I watched Cerro Roto and kept the topo map aligned with the land features. It was easier than the first trip because I had been there once and also because I was able to navigate while Susannah drove.

The terrain for most of the drive was rough—dunes, lava, arroyos, brush and cactus. About a mile before reaching the rim, the land rises slightly and flattens into a meadow. I guess that's where elk graze until someone puts an arrow into them. For those that survive the bow season, they have the guys with the big guns to look forward to later in the fall.

Susannah handled the truck like she'd been driving off road for years, which I suppose she had. When we reached the site, she maneuvered the truck into position as I directed.

I put my good foot in the loop on the bottom of the rope and slipped the rope though a safety harness around my waist.

"I don't think you should do this," Susannah said.

"You're the one who convinced me I should do it."

"I still think it has to be done. I just don't think *you* should do it. I think *I* should do it."

"I know. You're less squeamish than I am, you aren't afraid of heights and you don't have a cast on your leg."

"How did you know I was going to say that?"

"Because that's what Tristan said when he offered to do it."

"Well, he and I can't both be wrong."

"Okay, you're right. Either one of you is better suited for the task than I am. But this is not about who's best for the task. It's about who the task is best for. I need to do this."

She gave me a hug. "I'm proud of you."

"Hold the praise until we see what happens."

I took the shard out of my shirt pocket and stuck it in my back pocket so that it wouldn't break on the way down.

"Why are you taking that shard with you?"

"I'm sure it's an ancient body. After I verify that, I'm going to leave the shard in his hand."

"Why?"

"Because after I dismissed the idea of sticking a cross on his grave, I wondered whether something else would be appropriate. The shard is the best I can do."

I got down on my stomach and inched backwards until my foot and my cast were in midair. Susannah activated the winch, leaving about three feet of slack. I scooted back until my legs were over the rim and my torso still on level ground. The rope was taut.

"You can start letting it out very slowly," I said. "When it goes slack, you'll know I'm safely on the ground."

"Or came free from the harness and are in the bottom of the gorge," she said.

"Thanks."

The edge of the precipice had been worn smooth over the ages by the water that runs over it when it rains. Once my hips slipped over, all I had to do was keep my head up and my elbows out to avoid bumping my jaw when I went all the way over.

Then I closed my eyes and waited for my feet to make landfall.

Despite the cast, I managed to remain upright when I landed. I unhooked myself from the rope and looked around.

Nothing had changed.

I took the rebar out and started searching for pots. The soil wasn't compacted, so the iron slipped in easily every time I pushed it. I followed my usual grid pattern and spacing and hit only three things, all of which turned out to be rocks. No pots. Not even another shard.

Now it was time for the unpleasant part.

I moved the big stone and started digging with my gloved hands.

Thirty minutes later, I re-harnessed myself to the rope and gave it a tug. I heard the winch start. I looked straight up during the trip for two reasons.

First, I was afraid to look down.

Second, I needed to use my hands and arms to slip over the ledge with as few bumps and bruises as possible.

Once I was on high ground, I scrambled to my feet and unhooked the rope.

"Wind the rope up and let's get out of here," I said.

After we were moving she said, "I can tell from your voice and the look on your face that digging up that guy again really unnerved you."

I took a deep breath. "I didn't dig him up."

"You chickened out?"

"No. He wasn't there."

She slammed on the brakes.

"What do you mean he wasn't there?"

"There is no body down there. It's gone. Would you drive, please? I want out of here."

"I'm not going anywhere until we figure this out. Otherwise we'll just have to make another trip. Better to go back now and find the body."

"There is no body to find."

"You must have dug in the wrong place."

"I dug under the big stone that was right over the body. When I didn't find the hand at first, I figured I was off by a few inches, so I kept widening the hole. It got wider and wider until it was big enough to bury this truck in. I dug at least four feet in every direction."

"You didn't dig deep enough."

I shook my head. "I dug deeper."

She was thinking. I wanted out of there, but it was obvious she wasn't leaving until she had satisfied herself that the body really was gone.

"There's only one explanation. Someone moved the stone. You were digging in the wrong place."

I shook my head again. "You remember how you told me I should look for pots *before* I dug up the hand because once I touched the hand again I might be in no mental shape to look for pots?"

"Yeah."

"Well, I took your advice. I probed every square inch of the ground with my rebar using my six-inch grid pattern. And the bar sunk down with ease except for three rocks I hit."

I could see her relenting. "You're positive the body isn't there?"

"Absolutely. I've been digging pots for over twenty years. I know how to find things under the ground."

She slipped the truck back in gear and we started rolling.

Our tracks were still visible, so I didn't have to navigate. And she could go faster because she didn't have to wait for instructions. She was thinking as she drove.

When we hit the paved road, she said, "Here's what must have happened. Remember we considered the possibility that whoever took your Bronco wasn't stealing it but just wanted to strand you? It had to be the murderer. He saw the truck with the rope hanging over the ledge so he knew there was someone down there. He was afraid you would discover the body, so he moved the truck hoping you would die down there and his victim wouldn't be discovered. But when you made it out safely, he knew you might go to the police, so he had to move the body to another hiding place."

I had been thinking along the same lines. I didn't have a better theory, but I did see some flaws in the one she offered.

"Look, Suze, the place is difficult to get to. You just drove it round trip, so you know that. On my first visit, I arrived at dusk because I wanted to dig at night. So what was the murderer doing out there when he saw me?"

"I don't know. But someone who saw us driving across that rough terrain could ask the same question—what are those two idiots doing out here? We just have to assume he was there. We can find out the reason later."

"Okay, but if he wanted to kill me to keep me from finding his victim, why would he merely strand me? Stranding someone down there is not a death sentence. Even I got out, and I had a dog and wounded coyote to worry about."

She had to think about that one for a minute.

"Maybe he didn't strand you as a means to kill you but to preserve the opportunity. He didn't want to risk going down the narrow trail at night, so he stranded you knowing you wouldn't risk going *up* that trail at night either. Then he could lie in wait for you in the morning and kill you when you came up."

"But he didn't."

She shrugged. "Maybe he overslept."

"The theory has too many holes in it."

"So what's the alternative? It was just a hand, and your coyote was so hungry he came back and dug it up?"

"After moving a huge stone?"

"They're stronger than they look. Especially when they're hungry."

"I think we can ignore the coyote thesis for now."

"There is one person who knew you would be out there."

"Yeah, Alvar Nuñez. I thought of that, but it doesn't work. If he buried a murder victim down there, he never would have told me the location of the cliff dwelling in the first place. Not telling me is a lot easier and more effective than luring me out there and then trying to kill me. And while he must have been pretty certain I would go because of the interest I displayed in finding more pots like the one he brought, he had no way of knowing *when* I would go. We already said the place is so remote that the chances of crossing paths with someone out there are almost nil."

"Yeah, but you and your coyote met up, and what are the odds of that?"

"Can we just forget the coyote?"

"No need to be sensitive about it," she said.

"Sorry. I have to admit I can't think of any reason for someone to dig up and move the body unless he's trying to conceal a murder. But I can't see how to make that explanation fit with the Bronco being moved and me being out there. I think these events are unrelated. Someone buried a body there, got nervous that it might be discovered, and dug it up to put it in a better hiding spot. It was just a coincidence that it happened between my two visits."

"There are no coincidences, Hubert."

We drove along in silence. We were at a traffic light in Española when Susannah started laughing.

"What's so funny?"

"I figured it out. I know what happened. The key is the hole in the hand."

"How is that the key?"

"An angel came and rolled away the stone, and the body ascended into heaven."

I just stared at her.

"Well," she said, "it makes as much sense as any other theory, and at least there's historical precedence for it."

# 24

On the morning after my return from digging in an empty grave, Tristan drove me to my lawyer's club on the condition that he could order a *macchiato*. I told him ten in the morning was too early for a cocktail. He told me a *macchiato* is a coffee.

Layton Kent occupies a conspicuous table overlooking the eighteenth green. Layton is rather conspicuous himself, weighing in at three hundred pounds. Oddly, he doesn't seem fat, merely large. That look derives, in part, from his hand-tailored suits which fit so perfectly. You can't get those off the rack at the Big & Tall Shop.

His size is further masked by his being, for lack of a better word, sleek—slicked back hair, spa-smooth skin and manicured nails.

His other clients are the prominent and well-to-do of Albuquerque. He helps them shelter their wealth and defends them when they run afoul of the law. Unlike the Archaeological

Resources Protection Act, the laws his other clients break are 'white collar'. They do not dirty their hands in the honest toil of digging.

Nor are they ever arrested. When it is discovered that they have committed stock fraud or violated banking regulations, the matter is resolved in a conference room paneled with exotic wood species from an endangered rainforest. An agreement is worked out whereby they pay a small fine without admitting guilt. Then both sides repair to the club for drinks.

I am neither well-to-do nor prominent. Well, maybe I'm a bit prominent insofar as I have been arrested for murder a time or two, but that is not the sort of prominence that would qualify me to be a client of Layton Kent, esquire.

He stoops to represent me because his wife, Mariella, is a discriminating collector of ancient pottery, and I am her primary source for those goods.

She is also said to be descended from Don Francisco Fernandez de la Cueva Enriquez, *Duque de Albuquerque*, the man after whom our city is almost named. I say 'almost' because, as you may notice, the first 'r' is missing.

Like the body that was formerly above the Rio Doloroso.

I don't know where either one of them went.

In addition to being my best customer, Mariela de Baca Enriquez Kent is a socialite by virtue of her lineage, her money and—the only one that counts in my opinion—her class.

Tristan and I trailed Phillip, the captain, to Layton's table.

"These gentlemen claim to have an appointment with you, Mr. Kent," he announced in a tone that made it clear he doubted our claim.

"Thank you, Phillip. You may seat them and send someone to take their orders."

Layton then turned to us. "Hello, Tristan. It is a pleasure to see you again. I trust your studies are going well."

"Nice to see you, too, Mr. Kent. My studies are going well. Thanks for asking."

Instead of greeting me, Layton said, "You are fortunate to have this young man as your nephew, Hubert."

I agreed. The waiter arrived. Kent's club offers an array of specialty coffees. Their lattes are delicious. I ordered one with skim milk and no sugar. Not what I really wanted, but I was dieting.

Layton scrunched his nose on hearing my order but said nothing. He is normally a full cream and sugar man.

Tristan ordered his *macchiato*.

"An excellent choice," said Layton, "I think I'll have the same. The *macchiato*s here are not merely the espresso with a drop of milk offered by the chain coffee mongers. Our baristas place thick milk foam in a small cup then pour the espresso through the foam in a stream so thin that only a small dark spot shows on the foam. That, of course, is the *macchiato* that gives the drink its name."

"Ah, the mark," said Tristan. "I've read about it but never seen one done that way."

I feared they would soon be discussing the *macchiato*'s bouquet, its notes on the palate and the finish.

Layton asked me to explain my difficulty, and I did so.

He listened silently as he always does then closed his eyes.

After two or three minutes he said, "Hubert, you remind me of Braxton Goabling, a professor I had in law school. Goabling subscribed to the belief that the best way to prepare your mind for the ordinary was to exercise it on the extraordinary. He assigned bizarre cases for his students to analyze. You are my current Goabling. Except your cases are not pedagogical fictions. They are, contrary to all reasonable expectation, completely and shockingly real."

I doubt if he does this with other clients, but he often begins his analysis of my cases with a preamble of the sort just quoted. I do not comment on them.

"To summarize," he said, "while digging for pots on BLM property, you discovered a human hand which you took to be the hand of a prehistoric person. Not wanting to disturb the grave further, you covered the hand. Some days later, you began to wonder if the hand might belong to a contemporary person. I put aside the question as to whether the person in the ground was a murder victim as that issue has no bearing on your legal situation. You decided to return to the site for the purpose of examining the hand to determine the age of the body. But the body had been removed. You now seek advice on your legal liabilities and obligations."

I nodded.

"With regard to your first visit, the Native American Graves Protection and Repatriation Act contains a provision regarding the inadvertent discovery of a burial site. That provision specifies, and I think I am quoting precisely here, 'The person who makes the discovery must immediately notify the responsible Federal official by telephone and provide written confirmation to the responsible Federal official'. 'Immediate' is an imprecise term. You were stranded for two days and required medical attention after you were found. So I believe if you report the finding now to the BLM, they will judge you to be in compliance."

"Since they don't know when I was there, I could just tell them I found it yesterday."

"I will not comment on that suggestion. You would normally

have a legal obligation to report finding the grave. But the obvious legislative intent of that provision of NAGPRA is to allow the authorities to protect the remains. You now know that the remains are no longer there. Thus, the intent of the provision cannot be accomplished, rendering your reporting responsibility moot. You are required to report where a grave *is*, not where it *used to be*."

"So I don't have to report it."

"My legal opinion is that you are not required to report it under NAGPRA. But my personal opinion is that it would be an act of civic responsibility to inform them of it since knowing that there had been a grave there might be of some archaeological significance. If, on the other hand, the body you partially unearthed was a recent death, then you are required under New Mexico law to report it so that the authorities can record the death and attempt to discover its cause. But once again, the disappearance of the body may render that obligation moot as well. It is no more helpful to the State, perhaps even less so, than it is to the BLM to be told where a body *used to be buried*."

"It sounds like I don't have to report it either way."

"You should probably do so. But you have no legal obligation."

He could have saved the explanation and said only those last five words. But he charges by the hour.

"Can we talk about the pot now?" I asked him.

"May I see it, please?"

Tristan handed him the pot Martin Seepu had brought me. Tristan had become both my driver and my porter. I couldn't carry a pot and use crutches.

Kent lifted the pot into a beam of light and examined it.

"Mariela will like it. The price you mentioned on the phone

was five thousand. I had one of my paralegals withdraw cash as you requested."

He handed me an envelope. I opened it on my lap and counted it below table level.

I looked up and said, "There is only forty-five hundred in here."

He smiled. "I took the liberty of deducting my fee."

# 25

On the way back home, I gave Tristan sixteen hundred dollars to match the half of his tuition he'd saved from his summer job.

"I'll add it to the running total of what I owe you," he said.

I shrugged.

He took me to Dr. Batres' office where I paid my dental bill. Sharice was with a patient, so I didn't get to see her. I dealt with that disappointment by rationalizing that I preferred to envision her in her white dress rather than a blue lab coat.

Our next stop was at the pharmacy where I'd rented the crutches. I rented them only for three weeks because I was short of cash. Tristan ran in and paid enough to take me up to six weeks.

But not before he argued about it.

"Why are you renting crutches? There's a place that lets you use them for free."

"I know. That was the first place I called. Turns out you get to use the crutches free, but they say that for sanitary reasons, you have to buy the hand-grip pads and the armpit pads. Those pads were more expensive than renting."

"After six weeks of rental, you will have spent enough to have bought the crutches, much less the pads."

"I don't want to own crutches."

"Why not?"

"For the same reason I don't have life insurance. I don't want to prepare for things I don't want to happen."

Our final stop was the Old Town Savings Bank. This time I went in, releasing Tristan from his duties since the bank is within shambling distance from my house.

I paid my mortgage and met with a young woman named Saundra who had a small cubicle and a big customer-service smile. I told her I wanted to borrow some money using my equity in my building as collateral. She gave me a sheaf of papers to complete. I've never applied for a national security clearance, but it has to be easier than applying for a second mortgage.

When I got home, I placed the thousand dollars for Martin's uncle in my secret hiding place. Then I called Whit Fletcher, a detective with the Albuquerque Police Department, and asked him to drop by.

After shelling out for the tuition, dentist, crutches, mortgage and the money for Martin's uncle, I had just enough left from the forty five hundred to pay for the margaritas that evening.

But it was still early. I hobbled over to the Plaza and sat down on a shaded bench.

Although Layton's explanation had the ring of sophism, it was not for me to question. He said I had no legal obligation to report the body. I was off the hook. Legally.

But I didn't feel as good about it as I should have. Part of that may have been being broke. If I had found a couple of valuable pots high above the Rio Doloroso, I might have been fretting less.

But there was more to it than that. I was still worried about the dirt of the illegal antiquities trade rubbing off on me. And I felt guilty about missing Frank Aguirre's funeral. And maybe about Dolly, although it was clear that Dolly didn't think I had wronged her in any way.

"Hallow, Youbird."

That's the way it sounded. But I've gotten so used to it that I no longer think of it as an accent. It's just how Father Groaz sounds.

"Whot happen to your foot?"

Father Groaz is fluent in Latin, Spanish, French, Italian and his native Rusyn. Yes, Rusyn—not Russian. It's a Slavic language spoken in and around the Carpathian Mountains.

His English is fractured. Combine that with his booming bass voice, his thick beard and a black robe draped over a 6' 4" 250 pound frame, and you have someone right out of central casting if you're filming a vampire movie.

Inside that barrel chest beats a heart of gold. The parishioners love him, and even we non-Catholics in Old Town look to him for advice.

I told him how I sprained my ankle, including everything that led up to it.

"So I came out here to sit and think about the dead guy I accidentally unearthed."

I looked up at him. "I guess I came in search of spiritual guidance."

His deep-set eyes sparkled. "Then is a lucky coincidence that I come along. I am in that line of work."

"Susannah says there are no coincidences."

He stuck his hand into his beard and rubbed his chin. Or maybe he was petting a gerbil. That beard is its own ecosystem.

"She is correct *sub specie aeternitatis.*"

I thought about that. I'm not fluent in Latin even though I took four years of it. But that was decades ago. I attempted to read Spinoza in the original Latin three years ago to see if I had retained enough to do so. I got most of it, but it was hard work, so I gave up and switched to the English translation. Even in the English version, that phrase was still in Latin, as if it were one of those Latin terms we use every day, like *vice versa*, *alma mater* and *et cetera*.

But who uses *sub specie aeternitatis* in everyday English?

I knew it meant literally 'under the aspect of eternity'. But like many other phrases, the literal translation is probably not the real meaning. *Alma mater* literally means 'nourishing mother', but what it really means is the school we graduated from.

I didn't see how *sub specie aeternitatis* was related to coincidences, so I just set it aside and asked Father Groaz what I should do about the corpse.

"You should say a prayer of forgiveness."

"I did that immediately after I covered the hand and tamped down the soil."

"Should you also report it to the police?"

"I discussed that with my lawyer. He says I have no obligation to report it."

Groaz looked perplexed. "Why does he say this?"

"Because the point of reporting a body is so the police can dig it up, try to identify it and see if it died of natural causes or foul play. Since the body is no longer where I found it, that intent cannot be met."

"Hmm. You are satisfied with this advice?"

"I wouldn't be sitting here if I were."

"Perhaps you remember the Biblical story of David leading the hungry into the Temple to eat the holy bread on the Sabbath. David broke the laws of Moses, but Jesus said David was not wrong. You have to look beyond the letter of the law."

"So I should report it to the police?"

"I don't know. But you should learn from David. Do whot you think is right, Youbird."

"I will. As soon as I figure out what that is."

# 26

Fletcher showed up at four as we had agreed.

"Case you don't know it, Hubert, we cops are like doctors. We don't make house calls no more, so this better be something good."

I pointed down to my cast.

"You called me to report a broken foot?"

"It's not broken. It's sprained."

"It still ain't a police matter unless someone sprained it while assaulting you."

"I sprained it by accident, but that wasn't the point. The point is that I couldn't come to the police station because of this cast."

"We got ramps, automatic doors, little bells in the elevator to let you know what floor you're on, Braille tags, you name it. It's that accessibility law. A deaf and blind guy with no legs can make it in there."

Whit is not politically correct, and some would say he's a bit slack as regards 'to protect and serve'. I've known him a long time. He's relentless in going after the bad guys. His police procedures and his English are both occasionally improper, and he's been known to make a buck or two on the side when no one is likely to be damaged as a result of it.

"The reason I called you was I need to find out something about missing persons."

"Like what?"

"Like if there's one from a certain area."

He stood a little straighter. "What's this about, Hubert?"

"You know I don't dig in graves, right?"

"That's what you tell me."

"Well, it's true. But a lot of other pot hunters do. And one of them was recently surprised to find a body."

"Finding a body can't be much of a surprise to someone digging in a grave."

"The surprise was not the body. The surprise was that it wasn't prehistoric. It was someone who died recently."

"So you was out digging for pots and found a fresh corpse."

"It wasn't me."

"Right. It was a guy you know."

"Right."

"What's his name?"

"See, that's the problem. He told me about finding the dead guy because he wanted the police to know. But he doesn't want to get involved because he wasn't supposed to be digging in a prehistoric site. So I can't give you his name."

"Okay, Hubert, I'll play along. Where did this guy find the stiff?"

"I can't tell you that, either."

"What *can* you tell me?"

"The dead guy was probably from Taos or Rio Arriba County. Or maybe Sandoval. Maybe even Los Alamos."

"Well, that narrows it down."

I walked with him over to the pot I'd bought from Alvar Nuñez. I was getting better at using crutches.

"This pot was found in the same place as the body."

"Was it found *under* the body? Cause it's busted and most of it is missing."

"I don't know where it was found because I didn't find it."

"Right. The guy you know found it."

"No, it was found by a teenager."

"Let me guess—you don't know his name either."

"I don't. But it passed from the teenager to someone I do know named Alvar Nuñez. And Alvar sold it to me."

Whit looked at the card with the price on it.

"Three thousand dollars? The thing is just a couple of pieces glued together."

"Right. Think what one like it would bring if it wasn't broken."

"Gimme an idea, Hubert."

"Ten thousand dollars."

He let out a low whistle. "Are you trying to tell me there may be one like that where you dug up the dead guy?"

"A guy I know dug him up."

"Right. And that guy might be able to find a pot like that if he could clear up this dead guy thing?"

I nodded.

"Well why didn't you just say so in the first place?"

# 27

"Your reading is weird, Hubie. No one reads Spinoza, especially in Latin."

Martin had joined us at Dos Hermanas. He was having a Tecate. Susannah and I were having our usual margaritas.

"It was your suggestion, remember? You wanted me to read *The Burglar who Studied Spinoza* by that Block guy."

"And did you?"

"Part of it," I said weakly.

"And then you not only switched to the actual Spinoza, but in Latin to boot."

"I wanted to see if I could still read in Latin."

"And?"

"I eventually gave up and went to the English translation."

"And that's when you ran across 'subspecies eternity'. It sounds like a lower breed of animals that live forever."

Martin laughed. "It's not 'subspecies eternity'," he said. "It's *sub specie aeternitatis.*"

"Father Groaz used it to support your belief that there are no coincidences," I said.

She brightened. "Yeah? How so?"

"I didn't ask him."

"I can guess," Martin said.

"Give it a shot," said Susannah.

"To see something *sub specie aeternitatis* is to see it as God sees it, outside of time. Humans are in time. We change. Things around us change. What is true one day may not be true the next. But God is outside of time and unchanging. He sees things as they really are. So if you can see everything at once and not have to wait for it to unfold in time, there are no coincidences. Everything is part of a grand plan."

Susannah and I stared at him for a few seconds. We looked at each other. Then we looked back at him.

It was Susannah who finally spoke. "Two things," she said. "First, I can buy that everything is part of a grand plan. That's why I say there are no coincidences. But second, and more importantly, this is a bar, guys. This is not a place for theological discussions. This is a place to talk about booze, food, romance, sports and adventure."

Now it was Martin's and my turn to look at each other then back at Susannah and back at each other.

Martin spoke. "That's what theology is about—booze, food, romance, sports and adventure."

Susannah said, "I don't get it."

Neither did I. So I was happy that Martin spoke up.

"Theology is not about how many angels can dance on the head of a pin. Or at least it shouldn't be. It's about how to live. And life includes booze, food, romance, sports and adventure."

"Tell us about your tribe's theology," said Susannah.

He pulled a huge knife from his belt. "First we must have the blood ceremony," he said, deadpan.

"How about another Tecate instead," I said.

He placed the knife back in the sheath.

We signaled for Angie. Martin ordered his Tecate, specifying that he wanted it in a can. I ordered my usual margarita.

Susannah hesitated.

"Can you make a cucumber jalapeño margarita?"

Angie looked at her as if she were Father Merrin in *The Exorcist*.

"I've never heard of that," Angie finally said.

"I'm not surprised. It was invented by a friend, Stephanie Hunt Raffel."

Angie continued to stare at her.

"I'll have my usual," Susannah finally said.

After Angie left, I said, "What was that about?"

"I think we're in a rut, Hubie. My friend Stephanie served me a cucumber jalapeño margarita the other day and it was great."

"We're not in a rut. We're in a groove. I like my margaritas as they serve them here."

"Oh, yeah? Listen to this. You start by blending a peeled and seeded cucumber, a seeded jalapeño, lime juice, tequila, blue agave sweetener, and triple sec until the mixture it is smooth and frothy. Then you dip the rim of a glass into a combination of kosher salt, chile powder and *turbinado* sugar. Pour in the liquid, garnish with cucumber slices and top with a drizzle of Grand Marnier." She raised her eyebrows and waited for a response.

"That has to be a Santa Fe recipe. No one in the real New Mexico would do anything that fancy."

"But doesn't it sound good?"

I had to admit it did. I love cucumbers, jalapeños and margaritas. It just never occurred to me to combine them into one concoction.

I said to Susannah, "When I told you that Doctor Koehler introduced his hunting guide to me as Alonso Castillo Maldonado, you thought it was odd that he gave me all three names. But you just did the same thing for Stephanie Hunt Raffel."

"You're a bad influence on me. I told you people can't have two last names, and you said they aren't last names, they're Appalachians."

"'Appellations'," I corrected. "Or *apellidos* in Spanish," I added.

"Whatever. I don't know whether Hunt is Stephanie's middle name or one of those apple edos, so I used both Hunt and Raffel."

"Is she Hispanic?"

"How would I know?"

"You said she was your friend."

"She is, but we don't sit around talking about our ethnicity. Let's find another topic. If we continue on this one, you'll start explaining your Anthropological Theses."

The drinks came and Martin took us back to the subject of his tribe's theology.

He picked up his cold can of Tecate and blew on it. When his warm moist breath hit the cold surface, it condensed and swirled around the can.

"In the beginning there was only mist," he said dramatically and smiled. "Eventually, a wind moved through the mist. The wind separated the light from the dark. The light became the Holy

People. The dark became the serpents. Both the Holy People and the serpents were spirits. Nothing physical existed. The Holy People and the serpents started fighting. The Great Spirit, who we call *aeternitatis*, was unhappy and made them both physical. Their first dwelling place in the physical world was the Great Mesa. The serpents liked the great Mesa because they could come and go as they pleased. But the Holy People became thirsty because there was no water. So they left the Great Mesa and went to the canyons. They travelled at different speeds. Those who arrived first became men. The later ones became women. Because they were second, the women were made to bear children. The men ate of the ears of white corn and the women of the ears of yellow corn. Then the Coyote appeared and told them that each man should take a woman. If they did so, new Holy People would be created."

He stopped and took a sip of his fresh Tecate.

"Sheesh," said Susannah, "It's always the same. The women traveled slower. As a penalty, they were made to bear children. Then a dumb animal told the men to take a woman, as if we were fish from a trout stream."

"Makes sense to me," I said.

She threw a tortilla chip at me.

"I buy everything except the Great Spirit being called *aeternitatis*," I said.

"I changed that part. We are forbidden to translate our language."

"Really?" asked Susannah.

"Yep. Afraid you palefaces would mess it up."

"How did we get on this topic?" she asked

"We were discussing how God looks at things *sub specie aeternitatis*," said Martin.

"Yeah," I chimed in. "Which proves you're right—there are no coincidences. Everything is part of a grand plan. But humans don't know what the plan is. Things look like coincidences to us, but that's only because we are ignorant."

"Some of us more than others," she said, looking at me with a sly smile. "I don't understand why *sub specie aeternitatis* was in the English version of Spinoza's work."

"I guess the person who translated the book thought it's one of those Latin phrases we use, like *quid pro quo* and *carpe diem*."

Susannah shivered. "I've hated that phrase ever since I saw that film."

"I admit *carpe diem* is sort of corny," I said, "but I loved *Dead Poets Society*."

"I'm not talking about *carpe diem*. I mean *quid pro quo*. That creepy Anthony Hopkins used it in *The Silence of the Lambs*."

"I don't know why you watch scary movies," I said.

"Because they're better than reading Latin or talking about theology," she said, raising her glass.

Martin and I clinked it.

He started back to the Pueblo because he doesn't like to drive after dark.

"You think that's true about them not letting their language be translated?"

"I know it is. Ands it's easy for them to protect their language because they are the only Pueblo that speaks it."

She put her elbows on the table and clasped her hands together. "You remember a couple of years ago when the Santo Domingo Pueblo changed its name to Kewa Pueblo?"

"Yeah. I thought there was a subtle unintended message in that change. They got rid of the Spanish name *Santo Domingo* but kept the Spanish word *pueblo*."

She squinted. "The message is so subtle that I don't see it."

"The message is you can't change history. They have every right to take *Santo Domingo* off their signage, change the tribal letterhead and rename the tribal businesses, all of which they did. But it remains true that they were cruelly subdued by the *conquistadores* and spent four hundred years being known by a name that was not of their choosing."

"Maybe the name change makes them feel better about that."

"I hope so. But it won't change the facts."

"Because the facts are subspecies eternity," she said, laughing.

# 28

There is something odd about a man in his late forties being driven to a date by his nephew.

He offered to park and help me into the building, but that would have been even odder. It was only a few feet from the curb to the lobby then a short elevator ride to the 4th floor.

She greeted me with a lingering kiss on the lips. Not as lingering as the goodbye kiss on our first date but a step up from the kiss on the cheek I got on her first arrival. I took that as a good sign.

I reached into the cloth shopping bag I was carrying and handed her a bowl.

"This is for you."

She beamed but said, "I can't accept this."

"Sure you can. It's a present."

She shook her head. "When I first saw it in your shop, I also saw the price tag. I can't accept a thousand-dollar gift from you."

"This is not the bowl you saw. It's a copy."

She smiled. "So was that one."

"Yes. So this is a copy of a copy. Almost worthless."

"Nice try. It would bring the same price as the other one if you sold in your shop."

"Except I can't sell it."

"Why not?"

"Turn it over."

She did and read out loud the inscription I had carved before glazing and firing.

"To Sharice."

That earned me an even longer kiss.

"I should have brought a dozen more," I said, and she giggled.

She placed the bowl on the table and said, "I wish I had a stem of yucca."

Whereupon I reached into the bag and handed her one.

"You are amazing."

"Another kiss?" I asked. I'm shameless.

This was one longer still.

I looked forlornly into the empty bag and then up at Sharice. "I'm out of presents."

"Too bad. I'm not out of kisses."

I hope I didn't look like the lovestruck teenager I was feeling myself to be. I needed to look suave and debonair, if for no other reason than to fit in with the surroundings. Her apartment was in one of the new downtown condominium buildings and had floor to ceiling windows on the north wall overlooking Central a block away. The high ceilings had exposed steel beams with visible ductwork and electrical conduits. The floor was polished concrete, the counters black granite and the high-end appliances were stainless steel.

Although it was a small one bedroom unit, the clean open design made it look larger. The furniture was simple and functional, a black leather love seat, two Barcelona chairs and a glass coffee table. A larger matching glass table served as the dining table. A white table cloth was set with Fiestaware in the color the company insists on calling 'shamrock' but which is, according to the color chart I use for glazes, olive drab. I suppose it's a marketing thing.

Sharice put the bowl on the table, poured some water into it from a bottle of Pellegrino and stripped the yucca blossoms into the bowl. The fizz from the sparkling water made the blossoms dance around the bowl.

She wore a silver high-neck dress of crinkled chiffon with a slanting hemline. I don't know much about fashion, but the part of the dress that was modestly just above the knee made the other side seem tantalizingly short.

She had the same violet lipstick and eye shadow she had worn to my house. The lipstick was unfazed by the three kisses.

"You are an elegant woman," I said.

She twirled around. "You like?"

I thought she was referring to herself, but before I could frame a response, she said, "It's a Vera Wang. I think it makes me look stylish."

"I think you make the dress look stylish."

She retrieved a bottle of Gruet rosé from the fridge and asked me to uncork and pour.

"I thought the rosé would go well with the salad," she said. "I hope you don't mind having just a salad for dinner."

"I'm dieting, so a salad is perfect."

"You don't need to diet, Hubie."

"I feel like I need to, especially since this cast prevents me from walking."

"And from doing other things, too," she said mischievously.

"I could take it off."

"Good to know," she said. "Just in case."

The salad was frisee, cucumbers, tomatoes, avocados and fiddle-heads with a dressing of balsamic vinegar and maple syrup.

"I can taste something Canadian in the dressing," I said.

"And in the salad, too. Fiddleheads are popular in Canada."

"I've never seen them. I've never even heard of them."

"They're fern leaves picked before they unroll. I don't think ferns grow in the desert."

"Where do you buy them?"

"Whole Foods, but they get them only in the spring. I froze these, so they aren't quite as crisp as they should be,"

When we finished the salad, she said, "Sorry about your diet, but I do have dessert, and you aren't allowed to abstain."

I looked into her eyes and said, "Abstinence is the farthest thing from my mind."

She laughed and said, "Keep your cast on, cowboy."

When she told me it was saskatoon pie, I assumed it was named after the city, but it turns out that saskatoons are berries, sort of like blueberries. In Sharice's homemade crust—made, she assured me, with lots of butter—they were delicious.

She cleared the table, rejecting my offer to help on the grounds that I was sporting a cast. When everything had been taken off the table cloth, she removed it to reveal a Scrabble game board.

"Up for some fun and games?"

I resisted a tempting reply and said, "I love Scrabble."

She beat me in three straight matches, a 'hat trick' as she called it.

"Let's sit on the love seat and finish the bubbly," she suggested.

I sat on the loveseat and somehow she ended up on my lap. There ensued several minutes of serious mouth-to-mouth contact.

Then she said, "I'll drive you home."

"No need," I said. "After the last few minutes, I think I can fly."

She drove me home anyway and accepted my invitation to have dinner at my house again.

# 29

I awoke Sunday morning wrapped in warm memories of the evening with Sharice.

And in a light blanket. Fall had arrived early. It's always cool at night out here, but it had dipped into the fifties. Rather than close the door to the patio, I had opted for the blanket. I knew we would still have a few days in the eighties, maybe even in the low nineties, but there was color on the mountain and a nip in the air.

I cracked three eggs into a buttered ramekin, stirred in some salt, pepper and chopped jalapeños and put the ramekin in the oven. While that baked, I heated some leftover mole in a saucepan. I removed the eggs when the whites were set and the yolks warm but runny and poured the mole over them. Warm tortillas and cold Gruet completed the breakfast.

I opened the shop—all the merchants in Old Town open on Sunday. Except the ones who've gone out of business.

Among my other neuroses, I am mildly paranoid. I think the

media is hiding the truth from us. They keep saying the economy is recovering, adding little reservations like 'slowly' to make it seem more plausible. They report that unemployment is inching down.

What they don't mention is that unemployment statistics are based on the number of people registered at state employment offices as job seekers. When they give up and stop looking for work, they are no longer counted as unemployed. As Mark Twain said, "There are lies, damn lies and statistics."

The statistic in Old Town is that twenty shops have closed. La Hacienda, the competitor to La Placita where Susannah works, has shut its doors after more than sixty years in business. Remembering the many times I've stood on the east side of the Plaza looking across the street and trying to choose between La Hacienda and La Placita makes me sad. An era has ended.

The Memories in Old Town Gallery is also going out of business. It will now be merely a memory itself.

You can probably guess what I was wondering—will I be next?

But my evening with Sharice had me in such a good mood that I decided to throw a pot based on the Rio Doloroso shard. I propped the shard on a shelf in the workshop and began forming a piece with the same height and circumference. That was the easy part. The difficulty was duplicating the compound curve. It took so long I had to wet the clay a dozen times before I was satisfied.

I had the door to the shop open so I could see customers. I might as well have left it shut.

I closed around six and sat with Geronimo in the patio. Being outside always cheers me up as does being with a dog. They live in the moment. They don't worry about money or where their next meal will come from. Geronimo doesn't understand the word 'economics'.

He also doesn't understand 'stay' or 'fetch', but that's another issue.

He does, however, understand the vet's office, and he started moaning as we approached it the next morning in Tristan's car.

After I dragged him in—he seems to prefer being choked by his collar to being in the veterinarian's office—the vet, Julie, examined him. In spite of his appearance, she pronounced him fit.

Fit for what? I thought. But I kept silent because I didn't want to question her professional judgment or hurt Geronimo's feelings.

Julie looked at me as if I were also a canine patient and said, "You've recently had a sunburn. You want me to give you something to speed your recovery?"

"You can prescribe for humans?"

"I have a non-prescription cream you can use. It eases itching and stinging and speeds healing by diminishing moisture loss through the skin. It works just as well on humans as it does on dogs."

"Dogs get sunburned?"

She rubbed Geronimo behind the ears. "Not guys like this with full coats of long fur, but shorthaired breeds like Dalmatians and Greyhounds are susceptible. Of course the best treatment is prevention. You should always wear a hat."

"I know that. But mine disappeared."

She laughed and looked at Geronimo. "I'll bet you know where it is, don't you, boy?"

Then she looked back at me. "If he has a place he likes to dig or an area in some bushes, you might want to look there for your hat. Even male dogs have a nesting instinct, and they like to take soft personal items into their nests. It's a show of affection for their owners."

"I thought the phrase these days is 'human companion'."

"Dogs make good companions. I'm not sure humans deserve the term."

Then she depressed me by telling me about an abused Terrier she had recently treated. I covered Geronimo's ears so he wouldn't have nightmares.

# 30

The rule of thumb is that greenware should dry for two days.

But if your thumb is in high and dry Albuquerque, you can cut that in half. So the next afternoon I added the design to the pot. The pattern was beautiful in its simplicity. Bands of burnt sienna around the base and rim with a row of trapezoids around the belt that may well have represented corn kernels.

After finishing the design, I headed for Dos Hermanas.

"You smell weird."

Susannah is the only person I know who can be simultaneously blunt and charming.

Now that I think about it, maybe the unselfconsciousness of her bluntness is part of her charm.

"It's some cream the vet gave me for my sunburn," I explained.

"You go to a vet for sunburn?"

"You know I'm broke. A vet is cheaper than an M.D."

"That's the most ridiculous—"

"Just kidding. I took Geronimo to the vet. She noticed my sunburn and gave me the cream."

"She mistook you for a Dalmatian or a Greyhound?"

"How did you know those breeds get sunburned?"

"I was a pre-vet major."

She's had more majors than the Army.

She dipped a chip into the salsa and asked me to tell her about my date with Sharice. I was happy to do so.

"She lives in one of those pristine glass and steel condos downtown, all angles and hard surfaces."

"I don't get those places. They seem so cold. Plus they don't really fit with traditional New Mexico architecture."

"I like them better than the fake New Mexico architecture of the cookie-cutter suburbs. Sharice decorated hers to match the architecture, simple and clean. I guess it reflects her Canadian persnicketiness."

"Huh?"

"The label of my hat says it was handcrafted with Canadian persnicketiness."

"The hat's gone," she reminded me. "I'm not sure what persnickiness means," she added.

"Persnicketiness," I corrected, but stumbled over the last three syllables. "Hmm. I think your version of the word is better."

"What was she wearing?"

"A silver dress made of crinkled chiffon. It probably fit her so well because it was hand-tailored for her by a Chinese dressmaker."

"A Chinese dressmaker?"

"Yeah. Wong, Wee, something like that."

"Vera Wang?"

"That's it. You know her, too?"

"I don't know her and neither does Sharice. Vera Wang is a big-name *haute couture* fashion designer and a former ice skating champion. I'm surprised you haven't heard of her."

"Ice skating is not a popular desert activity, and I'm not into *haute couture*, whatever that is. I assumed she was some local seamstress."

Her shoulders sagged. "I'm not into *haute couture* either, but I know a lot about Vera Wang because she's the leading designer for wedding dresses. I think my mom has her on speed dial just in case I meet the right man."

Maybe she thinks you already have, I thought to myself.

"Did you take her flowers?" she asked.

"A stem of yucca blossoms."

"Did she strip them into a bowl like she did at your place?"

"Yes, into a bowl I made for her."

"That's a rather extravagant gift for a second date."

"She thought so too. She wanted me to take it back to the shop and sell it, but I told her she'd have to keep it because I couldn't sell it."

"Why not?"

"Because it was inscribed 'To Sharice'."

"You really like her."

"So much so it's scary."

"Be careful, Hubie."

"Thanks."

"What did she serve?"

"A salad of frisee, cucumbers, tomatoes, avocados and fiddleheads."

"Fiddleheads are a food?"

"It's a fern that grows in Canada. It reminded me just slightly of artichokes. The dressing had maple syrup in it."

"And for the main course?"

"The salad was the main course."

She laughed. "So that's how she stays so slim."

"Maybe it's how she justified the dessert, a saskatoon pie in a buttery crust."

"A Canadian-themed meal. And after dessert?"

"We played Scrabble."

"Scrabble is not 'chic', Hubie."

"It is when the board is revealed by removing the tablecloth, and the players are sipping Gruet rosé."

"And after Scrabble?"

"We smooched."

"Saying 'smooched' is so not 'chic'. Did it lead anywhere?"

"That's sort of a personal question, Suze."

"In other words, no."

We both laughed at that. "She said to me, 'Keep your cast on, Cowboy'."

"I guess it would be awkward with a cast."

"I don't think I'm likely to find out. But things are going great. Maybe after the cast is off . . ."

"Things are looking good for you."

I sighed. "Only in the romance department. The rest of my life is falling apart." I crunched a chip. "I'm beginning to wonder if there really is something to that King Tut Curse."

"You had nothing to do with King Tut."

I shook my head. "It's a generic term. Anyone who digs in a grave can get it."

"Good thing mosquitoes are rare in the desert," she joked.

"Dying from a mosquito bite is only one example. Curses can take any form."

"And what sort of curse are you suffering?"

"Think about it. Immediately after I dug in that grave, someone stole my Bronco. You say there are no coincidences, and I'm beginning to believe you. Then a coyote showed up dragging a chain. Doesn't that sound like some sort of macabre symbol?"

She was twisting a lock of hair around her fingers. "It is bizarre, but it doesn't necessarily have to be a symbol."

"Then I dropped my canteen and sprained my ankle, leaving me immobilized in the desert with no water, a potentially fatal situation."

"But you didn't die. You were rescued by a doctor even though you were in the middle of nowhere. That's the opposite of a curse. It's more like a miracle."

"Another way to look at it," I said, "is that it was just the curse keeping me alive so the next pestilence could be visited upon me. Like in the Old Testament. The only reason they didn't die of thirst during the drought was they had to be alive when the swarms of locusts arrived."

"Well, no locusts have shown up, and nothing bad has happened since you got back."

"Wrong. I got two bad phone calls today. The first was from a supercilious young woman at my bank saying they couldn't grant me a second mortgage."

"You've been paying on that place for over twenty years. You must have tons of equity."

"Equity is not the problem. I don't qualify for a loan because I have a low credit score."

"You don't pay your bills?"

"I don't have any to pay. The only bill I have is my mortgage, but they're the ones considering the loan so that doesn't count. What they want is a credit score based on how I've paid other people."

"What about your credit card?"

"I rarely use it. And when I do, I pay it off when the statement arrives."

"That should help raise your credit score."

"No. It lowers it."

She plunked her glass down on the table. "Paying off your credit card *lowers* your credit score?"

I nodded. "I know it sounds crazy, but if you pay the whole balance, then you really don't have a loan from the credit card company. They were just a sort of payment agent for you. But if you make installment payments and have a rotating balance, then your credit score goes up because you are handling the loan responsibly."

"No you're not. The responsible thing is to pay it and avoid interest."

"Yeah," I agreed, "if you want to be responsible to yourself. But the bank can't make money that way."

"So they reward you for paying them interest by giving you a higher credit score so you can qualify for a loan and then . . . wait, pay them more interest. I guess it does make sense—for the banks. And I suppose this system was invented by the same crooks who ran the banking system off the cliff then got a government bail-out."

"You got it. And then used some of our money to give themselves huge bonuses."

"This is making me mad. Let's change the subject and go to the second bad call. Maybe it will be better."

"Huh?"

"But first," she said, "let's get another round."

I agreed we had earned it by breaking the code to our evil banking empire even though there was nothing we could do about it, so I signaled Angie for replenishments.

After they arrived, I told Susannah what Whit Fletcher told me.

"He said he'd poked around, and there is no missing person who's a likely candidate to be our friend from the cliff dwelling."

"How would he know that?"

"He called his connections with the sheriff's offices in each of the counties closest to the site. They told him the people they have on their missing list are people they suspect have relocated of their own volition, people running out on child support or skipping bail, things like that. Then there are a few missing children. There is no adult they are actively looking for."

She mulled it over. "I guess it was worth a try, but it doesn't tell us much. The dead guy could have been a drifter, an illegal immigrant or some other type who wouldn't be on any record."

"Like a prehistoric person," I said. "They didn't record deaths in the tenth century."

"It's not a mummy, Hubert. Someone moved it, remember? You agreed that means it was probably a murder victim. You got too close to the evidence, so the killer relocated the body."

"I did think that made sense, but there's another possibility. Maybe a treasure hunter found the body and took it."

"Why?"

"To sell, of course. Human remains bring big bucks on the black market."

"God, that is so sick."

# 31

The pot went into the kiln the next morning.

I was happy with what came out that afternoon. It wasn't exactly like the shard, but it was close enough to fool the average buyer.

Not that I deliberately set out to deceive buyers, average or otherwise.

If someone is conceited enough to think he knows a genuine work when he sees it, being hoodwinked is just reward. But when a buyer asks me if a pot is genuine, I tell the truth.

After it had cooled, I took the pot to the shop and placed in on a shelf. I looked at it trying to decide on a price. Then I glanced at the partial pot Alvar Nuñez had brought, and lightning struck.

It wasn't the electrical kind from the sky. It was the mental kind from your brain when the synapses line up and truth strikes you like a bolt out of the blue.

The pot Alvar sold me was not from that cliff dwelling high above the Rio Doloroso.

I've been studying pot designs for over twenty years. There was no way the people who produced that shard also produced that pot. The designs were too different. To think they came from the same tribe would be like thinking Lew Wallace wrote both *Ben-Hur* and *The Da Vinci Code*.

I examined the Alvar pot closely.

I paced the floor until a quarter to five, no mean accomplishment with a cast on my foot. Then, I started my walk to our watering hole.

"Alvar Nuñez is a fraud," I said after taking the first sip of my margarita. "That pot he sold me didn't come from the cliff dwelling."

"How do you know?" Susannah asked.

"It doesn't match the shard I found there."

"It doesn't have to, does it? Not all pots made by the same tribe are alike."

"Right. But there are certain consistencies in the designs, shapes and colors. Even casual collectors can tell the difference between a piece from Acoma and one from Kewa."

"And the shard and the pot are that different?"

"Worlds apart."

"Wait," she said excitedly, "maybe the pot is from the cliff dwelling and it's the shard that isn't."

I shook my head. "I dug up the shard myself, so I know it was from there."

"You also dug up a hand, and it wasn't from there."

"Why would someone bury a shard there?"

"Maybe the dead guy had it on him when he was killed."

Oh brother. "We don't know for certain that he was murdered. And even if he was, the shard is the ringer, not Alvar's pot. I examined it closely after I realized how different it is from the shard. Not only didn't his pot come from that cliff dwelling, I don't even think it's Anasazi. I think it's a very good fake."

"Maybe it's one of yours," she said and laughed.

"I can't believe I bought a fake."

"I'm glad you did. This could help us solve the mystery."

"Which mystery is that? Who stole my Bronco? Who moved the body? What happened to my hat?"

"The first two. Forget the hat. Tell me everything Alvar said to you."

I closed my eyes and tried to remember our conversation.

"He said he got the pot from a teenager who said he found it in a cliff dwelling." I hesitated because that didn't sound right. "No, what he actually said was, 'I got it from a teenager who knows about an ancient cliff dwelling near our village'."

"So he didn't actually say the pot came from the cliff dwelling."

"Not in so many words, but why mention the cliff dwelling if the pot didn't come from it?"

"Tell me about the rest of the conversation."

She loves this stuff.

"When he told me he got the pot from a teenager who knows about an ancient cliff dwelling, I asked him where, and he said at his house. I said I meant where was the pot *found*, not where did he get it. He ignored that question. He said he would take two thousand for the pot. I offered him five hundred. Then he said if I gave him a thousand he would also tell me where the cliff dwelling is."

She chewed on that while I loaded a chip with salsa.

"So he asks for two thousand. After you counter with only five hundred, he goes all the way down to a thousand without further haggling. And he throws in the location of the cliff dwelling even though he had ignored your earlier request for the location."

I nodded.

"So he doesn't haggle much, takes a low price and throws in the location. It's obvious, Hubie. He wasn't there to sell a pot. In fact, the pot wasn't even from the cliff dwelling. He just let you believe it was to make to make the cliff dwelling even more interesting to you. His goal was to lure you to that cliff dwelling."

"If he was using the pot to lure me to the cliff dwelling, why not just say flat out that it came from there?"

"We can answer that question after we answer the more important one."

"Which is?"

"There's only one reason why he would want to lure you there—he wanted you to find the body."

"Why would he want me to find the body?"

"Exactly. That's the important question we have to answer."

We sat in silence except for the crunching of chips. I finally said I couldn't think of any reason why he would want me to discover the body. I was not surprised that she had thought of several.

"He's the murderer and subconsciously wants to be caught because he can't handle the guilt."

"Then why not just go to the police? Why involve me?"

"Maybe his guilt is not about the murder. Maybe he thinks the victim had it coming. But he still feels guilty about burying him in an Anasazi site."

"You're striving."

"Yeah, you're right. How about this? Alvar is not the murderer, but he knows who is. He wants the guy caught."

"Same issue. Why not just go to the police?"

"I've got it! You told me he lives in a tiny village. That means he knows everyone there. The murderer is a dangerous guy. Alvar is afraid if he goes to the police, the murderer will come after him. But if it looks like an accidental discovery, the murderer won't connect it to Alvar."

"I don't know, Suze. Seems a bit far-fetched."

"So maybe we don't know the reason. But you admit it looks like Alvar wanted to lure you to that site."

"I admit that could be the case."

"Then the best way to find out why he did it is to ask him."

# 32

We left for La Reina the next morning.

The trip took us 3,000 feet up in elevation and 300 years back in time.

A primitive road snaked along a creek and eventually up to the spring which was its source. It was a good thing Susannah hadn't yet traded the truck back for her Crown Vic. That boat would have struggled climbing the dirt road to La Reina, a village time has forgotten.

The villagers seemed to like it that way. Low adobes were scattered around a system of *acequias* that fed level plots of corn, beans and chiles and small orchards of apples and apricots. The road ended in a *placita* around which were clustered a café and bar named El Erupto del Rey, a general store, a gas station, a town hall, a hair salon, a grocery store, two empty stores and a church, the only building in town that wasn't eroding.

The café had booths against the front wall, tables in the center of the room around an open area for dancing and a bar along the back wall with a dozen stools. We sat on the stools and asked the kid behind the bar what they had to eat. He said they had pizza, hamburgers, tacos and chile stew. Susannah chose the hamburger. The smell of roasting chiles hanging in the air forced me to chance the stew.

The kid threw a hamburger patty on the grill along with the two halves of the bun face down. He spooned some stew from a crockpot into a bowl. The crock-pot seemed out of place, but so did a fifteen-year-old barkeep.

"You want a beer?" he asked.

"You're not old enough to serve beer."

He shrugged. "There's no one else here."

"You have Corona?"

"Sure."

"Okay, I'll have one."

He had a pleasant kid's smile. "You're not a policeman, are you?"

"I'm not."

He opened my beer and Susannah's Pepsi. He flipped the patty, dressed the bun like he'd been working as a short-order cook for years and slid a standard hamburger onto the bar.

"I suppose you know everyone around here." I said.

"Yeah."

"I'm looking for a guy named Alvar Nuñez."

He shook his head.

"You sure?" I asked.

"There's only eight *apellidos*—family names—around here."

Susannah shot me a glance at the word *apellidos*.

"What are they?" I asked.

"Zaragosa, Maldonado, Campos, Castillo, Padilla, Gomez, Medrano and Maestas."

"How come you can list all the names so easily?" Susannah asked him.

"My great grandmother made me memorize them. Those are the eight *apellidos* of the families on the original land grant."

"And everyone here is descended from those families?"

"Some married in from outside, but they got the old names when they married. Except for a white guy named Braddock. I don't know when he came here. He's married to one of my aunts."

"Is there anyone else I could talk to?"

"My great grandmother is here, but she doesn't speak English."

"I speak Spanish. I'd like to meet her."

He shrugged and passed through a curtain in a doorframe. When he came back he said, "She wants to know what you want to talk to her about."

"I want to ask her about someone from La Reina who may be missing."

After another consultation, he motioned me to follow him to the back. When Susannah rose, he said, "Please wait out here, Miss."

The young man introduced his great grandmother, who called him Ernesto, as Señora Celerina Gomez Maestas. He didn't give her my name since he didn't know it. I introduced myself and thanked her for agreeing to speak to me.

After a bit of polite conversation, Ernesto brought us coffee. After we had finished the coffee, I told her a scientist who was studying the Rio Doloroso had found an unmarked grave, at which news she crossed herself and kissed her rosary.

I asked her if she had heard tales of people being buried in unmarked graves either in the past or recently. She said all the villagers were strictly traditional with regard to burials, and she was sure no one in the area had been buried anywhere other than the cemetery by the church. I asked her if there had ever been runaways or disappearances. She said some people left, of course, mostly young people. They went to the big cities like Taos or Tierra Amarilla for the excitement.

I managed to keep a straight face.

I asked her if she knew anyone named Nuñez. She did not. Then, on a hunch, I asked if there might be someone who could contact the spirit of the person in the unmarked grave.

Her eyes seemed to withdraw under her wizened brow. She crossed herself again and said, "*Claro que sí, la curandera.*"

# 33

"So we're going to wait around until the *curandera* shows up, and then what? Have a séance?"

"Maybe. Or maybe just get some information. *Curanderas* know a lot about their villages."

We had moved from the bar to one of the booths. The lamp over the table—an inverted T with a metal cylinder on each end—cast a yellow cone of light over each of us. I felt like I was sitting in a comic book frame.

"Hubie, I need to start learning a few words in Spanish. I'm going to the bar for a fresh Pepsi. This one is warm."

I turned to look at Ernesto's replacement. He was a handsome young man with deep-set dark eyes.

"How do you say 'eyes' in Spanish," she asked me.

Just as I suspected. She wanted to flirt with the new bartender, tell him he had beautiful eyes.

"*Ojos*," I answered.

She went to the bar, got a fresh glass of Pepsi, chatted up the young man and returned to the booth.

"I saw you flirting with the bartender."

"He does have great eyes, but I wasn't flirting with him. While he fixed my refill, I asked if he knew anyone named Nuñez."

"Does he?"

"He says he doesn't. Do you think Nuñez really doesn't live here or are the villagers just protecting him?"

"I don't think Ernesto could lie so convincingly. Same for his great grandmother."

"What address was on his drivers license?"

"I looked at his license to verify his name. I didn't look at the address."

"Why would he tell you he lives here?"

"I have no idea." I thought for a moment. "Do you think it might have something to do with why Señora Gomez didn't want you to be there when she and I talked?"

A wide smile spread across her face. "I don't think Señora Gomez knows I'm here. It was Ernesto who wanted me to stay out here."

"Why?"

"So he could hit on me."

"You have got to be kidding. He's only about fifteen."

"He says he's eighteen. He asked me if I was married. When I told him I wasn't, he asked me for a date."

"And where does one go on a date in La Reina?"

"Right here. We're having dinner and then we'll do some dancing."

"Have you lost your mind?"

"Lighten up, Hubert. He's a nice kid. Innocent. He probably just wants to have his friends see him with a woman. Plus, there will be a chaperone."

"His great grandmother?"

"No, you."

My mouth opened, but it evidently had nothing to say, so it closed.

"And you won't be alone," she said. "He's arranged for you to have a date as well."

"Oh, no. I appreciate you driving me up here, and I'll go along with boosting Ernesto's ego, but I am not going on a blind date in La Reina, and that is final."

While I was talking, Susannah was watching something behind me. I heard footsteps. A woman about Susannah's age appeared at our table.

"Hubert, I'd like you to meet Ernesto's sister, Sirena."

Her name was well-deserved, a *femme fatale* who could lure sailors—or pot thieves—with her enchanting voice.

"*Hola, Huberto. Ernesto me dijo que habla español,*" she said in a throaty voice. She sounded like an Hispanic Hepburn.

"*Un poco,*" I said, stupidly. I probably speak Spanish better than she did, but her appearance flustered me. She was like a *tamale*, delicious but not good for you, a burgeoning young woman in a sheaf of a dress that couldn't quite contain her assets. This is why men behave like idiots, I said to myself.

The bar had begun to fill as the day ended and people gathered to unwind. We sat in the booth—Susannah and her precocious boy toy on one side, me and my fellow chaperone *cum* temptress on the other.

A plate of *carnitas* appeared. Beers showed up on the table. The jukebox played. Susannah and Ernesto danced, he holding her like a life raft.

What the hell. I took Sirena's hand and we waltzed to the strains of Freddy Fender.

*Si te quiere de verdad*
*Y te da felicidad*
*Te deseo lo mas bueno por los dos*
*Pero si te hace llorar*
*A mi me puedes hablar*
*Y estaré contigo cuando triste estas*

The last line in Spanish translates, *I'll be there when you are sad.* The English is better, *I'll be there before the next teardrop falls.*

I guess they changed it to make it rhyme, but it lost something in the translation.

She smelled of baby powder and hair spray. She came easily into my arms and put her head on my shoulder. I was not tempted in the least. It was a party. In the arc light of the moment, we were performers on a stage, nothing more.

We returned to the table when *No Seas Cruel* started playing. I like Fender's Spanish rendition of the old Elvis hit, but I don't know how to dance to it.

The place was now overflowing, in part because every teenager was there watching Ernesto and Susannah dance.

Not a few of them and some of the older patrons as well were giving me strange looks. Not looks of hostility or even curiosity. More like admiration mixed with concern.

Ernesto's replacement as barkeep was named Baltazar. I thought of him as Baltazar *de los ojos* as he approached our booth.

"Sirena," he said, "Hugo is on his way."

Baltazar walked away. Sirena seemed frozen in place.

"Sirena," I said, "who is Hugo?"

"*Mi novio*. But he don't use 'Hugo'. He use his nickname."

"Which is?"

"*El Bastardo*."

Wonderful. I was the blind date for *El Bastardo*'s girlfriend.

"Tell Susannah I'll wait for her in the truck," I said, abandoning my chaperonal duties.

But it was too late. *El Bastardo* was charging into the bar, his biceps bulging from his muscle shirt and his eyes doing the same from his bulldog face.

He reached the table just as I was swinging my leg out to make a getaway. My cast crashed against his shin, and he winced in pain, giving me time to scramble to my feet and stand on the bench seat of the booth, the only surface available at the moment. He leaned in and took a swing at me. I arched back to avoid the blow and lost my balance. My head hit the wall, my butt hit the bench and my legs shot out from me like battering rams.

The cast delivered a second blow to Hugo, this time in a location considerably more painful than the shin. He dropped to his knees and moaned, but he was still blocking my way. I tried to clamber over the table to get past him on the other side of the booth. He recovered while I was doing so and his head came up to table height just in time to intercept the leg I was swinging across the table. There was a sickening crack as the cast caught him full force on the side of his head. He dropped to the floor unconscious.

I scanned the room. It was like a photograph. No motion, no sound. Then they all rushed at me. The strange thought that streaked through my jumbled brain was that dying of thirst would have been better than what was about to happen.

They closed in on me, their arms extended.

And patted me on the back. And cheered. And dragged me to the bar and started pouring me shots of mescal.

# 34

I must have passed out. The first thing I saw the next morning was a poodle skirt.

Above the skirt was a pink sweater. Above that was the face of a girl about eight years old.

"He's awake," she yelled, sending needles through my brain. Three other girls the same age rushed in to see the strange man on the couch.

The first girl, evidently the ringleader, pointed to my cast. "This is his weapon. He used it to beat up *El Bastardo*."

They took a step back. Then they giggled and ran out of the room. I lifted my head and the needles returned. I scanned the room moving nothing but my eyes. Even my eye muscles hurt.

The couch was upholstered in heavy brocade. The ceiling was pressed tin. I could see a lamp shade beyond my cast. It was yellowed and had beads hanging from it. There were scores of photographs on the wall. They seemed to comprise a family history.

Or maybe a village history. Some were so old they might have been daguerreotypes, their subjects dressed in nineteenth century garb and standing next to wagons, mules and hand-guided plows.

I heard footsteps but dared not move my head to see what was coming. A dark and diminutive ancient woman placed a chair next to the couch and introduced herself as La Viuda de Cheche Zaragosa Medrano, meaning the widow of Cheche Zaragosa Medrano. She explained that the crowd from El Erupto del Rey had brought me to her house because I had earlier expressed a desire to meet with the *curandera*.

She handed me a cup of hot liquid I assumed to be coffee until I drank it and discovered it was an herbal tea. She assured me it would cure my hangover. I was skeptical. But thirty minutes later I was sitting at her kitchen table eating eggs and tortillas and drinking my third cup of the strange brew that tasted of *epazote*, *estafiate* and *yerba buena*.

It was better than it sounds.

I asked about Susannah.

"She was with the others who brought you here. I did not allow her to stay because I fear she is a *bruja*."

The thought of Susannah being a witch made me laugh, but a hard glare from the deep-set eyes of *La Viuda* silenced me.

We talked for two hours while the little girls continued to run about the house occasionally peeking around the doorway to get a glimpse of me as if I were the bearded lady or the two-headed calf.

I asked her about Alvar Nuñez and got the same response everyone else had given.

I asked her about wandering souls. She told me there were many. I asked if there had been a new one recently.

"Yes, but I do not know who. When someone from his family comes to me, I will know it."

I thought about lining up all the people in and around La Reina and parading them by *La Viuda*. I dismissed the idea because the logistics seemed too complicated, and I couldn't imagine them agreeing to it anyway. Not to mention that I wasn't all that sure she could identify wandering souls.

But if being a wandering soul is just the hangover of death, then she could probably do it. Mine was completely gone.

My next to last question was about anyone who may have left La Reina in the last year or so. She said young people leave every year.

"But most of them return to visit," I noted, "I want to know if there are any who have left and not come back."

After thinking about it, she said there were only three: Hector Zaragosa Maldonado, Carlos Campos Castillo and Jesus Padilla Gomez.

Or maybe their names were Hector Campos Gomez, Jesus Zaragosa Padilla, and Carlos Maldonado Castillo. It's a good thing I wrote them down.

My final question was whether she knew where Susannah had gone. She told me Señora Celerina Gomez Maestas had taken Susannah back to the bar where she could spend the night with her and Ernesto.

# 35

Traversing the fifty yards from La Viuda's home to El Erupto del Rey took a full ten minutes because I had to hunt for a safe spot to brace the crutch tips with each step.

One of Susannah's interests in art history is the religious folk art found in New Mexico's old adobe churches. I also like the work of the *santeros*, but it is the buildings themselves that intrigue me, especially the small unpretentious ones constructed by the local faithful. There are 362 catalogued old adobe churches in the state, most of which were built before the United States existed and many that are badly deteriorated. Thankfully, the Archbishop's Commission for the Preservation of New Mexican Churches is working with Cornerstones Community Partnerships and other organizations to save these historical treasures. Two of my favorites are the Old San Ysidro Church in Corrales with the unusual metal pyramidal caps on its buttresses and the Saint Francis de Paula Church in Tularosa with its massive front wall in gleaming whitewash.

I was not surprised that Susannah wanted to visit the local church before we left. Its thick adobe walls were coated with traditional clay plaster and supported by rounded buttresses. The front door was rough-hewn pine. It must have weighed two hundred pounds, but it swung open easily. A central aisle ran between gigantic log pillars that rose thirty feet to the ceiling. There were pews between the pillars and walls. There were no windows. A small light behind the chancel was the only source of illumination. Niches in the walls contained the Stations of the Cross. The altar was made of tin and brightly painted.

I sat in one of the pews enjoying the cool still air as Susannah examined the work of the artisans in the niches.

She returned to me and said, "I think I'll make confession."

"Good idea. You need forgiveness for corrupting the youth of La Reina and practicing witchcraft."

"Practicing witchcraft?"

"Yeah, that's why La Viuda de Cheche Zaragosa Medrano wouldn't let you stay in her house. She said you're a *bruja*."

"Why would she think that?"

"Maybe because of the way you beguiled poor innocent Ernesto."

She shrugged, stepped over to a confessional and closed the door behind her.

From my seat in the near dark and behind one of the pillars, I watched the priest emerge from his office and enter his side of the booth. He wore the *cappa nera* of the Dominicans. They were not in there long, which I took as a good sign. I watched the priest intently when he returned to his office.

I met Susannah outside.

"Ready to go?" she asked.

"Not quite. I'm also going to make a confession."

She looked understandably perplexed. "You're not Catholic."

"That's why you have to give me a few pointers."

I asked several questions, the last one being how the priest would know to come out from his office. I didn't want to sit in the booth for hours waiting. I'm claustrophobic.

"They just know, Hubie. They have holy powers. I'll meet you at the truck in front of the bar."

The holy power in this case was a string attached to the door and running through a hole in the wall, probably to a bell in the office.

When it came time to do so, I said "Bless me, Father, for I have sinned. It has been over thirty years since my last confession."

"We can talk of that shortly. What do you wish to confess?"

"I was digging illegally for ancient artifacts and discovered a human body."

There was a long silence.

"Where did this happen?"

"In a cliff dwelling over the Rio Doloroso."

After another long silence, he said, "Please step out to the pews."

We walked over to them. He gestured for me to enter. I sat down a few feet from the end, leaving him a place which he took.

He said, "I think it best that we continue this conversation outside the protection of the confessional. Do you object?"

"No."

"Did you report the body to the police?"

I shook my head.

"Why not?"

"I thought it was the remains of a prehistoric person, a mummy so to speak."

"But you have changed your opinion?"

"Yes. A friend whose opinion I value believes the body is a contemporary person. She and I analyzed and debated it. I won't bother you with the details. The upshot was that I decided to go back and examine the body to determine whether it was ancient or modern. But the body was no longer there. It had been moved."

The priest sat in thought, his thumbnail under his front teeth.

"What do you deduce from the absence of the body?" he finally asked.

"My friend believes the missing body proves it was a contemporary person. One who was murdered. The murderer knew I had discovered the body so he moved it to cover his crime."

"And what do you think?"

"I think it remains possible that it was prehistoric."

"If that is so, there would be no motive for its removal."

"I'm afraid there could be. It would not be to conceal a murder. It would be for profit. Mummies are in great demand in the illegal antiquities trade."

He shook his head slowly and stared down at the floor. Perhaps he was in prayer.

"What steps have you taken since discovering the body has been moved?"

"I talked to my lawyer and my priest."

He smiled. "In that order?"

"Yes. Sorry."

He waved it off. "What did your lawyer advise?"

"He said the purpose of the law requiring the reporting of a body is so the police can investigate. Since I no longer know where the body is, that purpose cannot be met. So I have no legal obligation to report the initial discovery."

"And your priest?"

"He said I should ignore the letter of the law and do what I think is right."

"Always sound advice. May I ask his name?"

"Father Groaz."

"A diocesan priest. I often think they are closer to the people than we religious priests."

"Shouldn't all priests be religious?"

He laughed. "Unfortunately, some are not, as the world has recently discovered. But I wasn't using the term in that way. A 'religious priest' is one who belongs to an order and has taken the three vows—poverty, obedience and celibacy. Diocesan priests are bound only to celibacy, although they are in fact obedient and rarely wealthy."

"How did you know Father Groaz is a diocesan priest?"

"Because there is no saint named Groaz. When we enter the orders, we take a new name, and it must be the name of a saint."

"What name did you choose?"

"Jerome."

"So," I asked him, "shall I call you Father Jerome or Alvar Nuñez?"

# 36

It was now his turn to confess.

"It started in that booth," he said, waving a hand in the direction of the confessional. "A parishioner told me he had committed two sins. The first was participation in the dark rites of the Penitentes. You are aware of this sect?"

I nodded. Like most people who grow up in New Mexico, I heard tales of the Penitentes but had little factual knowledge.

"The second thing he confessed was witnessing a death at the cliff dwelling, a location they use to ensure they will not be discovered or interrupted. He sought forgiveness for his failure to report the death."

"He didn't tell you who the victim was?"

Alvar—Father Jerome, I still didn't know what to call him—let out a long sigh as if he had been holding his breath. "No. I wish he had. I struggled with this information for several weeks, trying, as your Father Groaz advised you, to ignore the letter of the law and do what I think is right. But like you, I was hesitant and unsure."

"I know information received in confession is sacrosanct," I said, "but couldn't you have reported the fact of the death to the police without revealing who had told you?"

He let out another sigh and shook his head. "I could have done that. But I had to consider the consequences. I didn't want the police trying to extract confidential information from me or my parishioners. Being questioned aggressively by the police would hardly qualify me as a martyr. My larger concern was my parishioners."

He looked up at me. "The Penitentes were virtually in control of this parish when I arrived. The deacons and I have made great strides to reduce their influence. Their *morada* is gone. Their number is reduced. They have been driven underground. The last thing we need is the police questioning the parishioners. Everyone would suspect that I had tipped the police about the death. Even though I would have withheld the name, it would destroy their confidence in me and, more importantly, the Church. I also did not want the police trying to discover who made the confession, pitting neighbor against neighbor, child against parent. It would tear this community apart. And yet . . . it did not seem right simply to remain silent. The deceased person deserved better than an anonymous grave. His family deserves to know his fate. The people who participated in his death—I will not quite call it a murder—should be called to account for their actions."

"So you decided to come to me."

He nodded. "I remembered a newspaper article about you in which you were described as someone who has long been suspected of illegally digging up old pots. The article caught my attention because of its unusual headline, *Pot Thief with a Conscience?*"

"I remember that article," I said. "I had returned some sacred pots to the San Roque Pueblo. I did it because it was the right thing to do. The last thing I wanted was publicity."

"I thought it was a perfect compromise," he said. "If you found the body and reported it, then the authorities could identify the victim, notify his family and arrange for a proper burial. And this community would be spared an ordeal. But compromises are never perfect. By involving you, the villains discovered their misdeed was known. They have moved the body. Now it will never be found."

"You have no idea where they might have taken the body?"

"No." He looked down and shook his head. "My meddling has only made things worse." He looked back up at me. "I'm sorry to have involved you in this sordid mess."

"No apology necessary. I'm sorry I didn't go directly to the police as my friend suggested."

A slight smile formed on his lips. "Over thirty years since your last confession?"

"Yes, and the person who heard it was not Catholic."

"Nor, I would hazard, are you."

I admitted it. Then I said, "I have a question for you. Since you've taken a vow of poverty, how did you have the money to pay the teenager for the pot you sold me?"

"I never said I paid him. I said I *got* it from him. He brought it to me out of gratitude for helping him recover from a drug habit. We are not supposed to receive gifts other than small tokens such as cookies or a bottle of inexpensive wine. I know those rules exist for a legitimate reason. Personally, I find poverty to be spiritually liberating. But it is socially awkward to refuse a gift from a parishioner, especially one as fragile as this young man. So I accepted the gift, knowing I couldn't keep it. When I hit upon the plan involving you, it was also an opportunity to divest myself of the pot in what I thought was a good cause."

"I should have known something was fishy when you didn't bargain hard and also threw in the location of the cliff dwelling."

"I have no experience in such matters."

"What did you do with the thousand dollars I gave you?"

He smiled. "I told the teenager and his mother that I enjoyed having the pot but had to sell it because we are not supposed to become attached to material goods. That was easier for both of them to accept than turning it down when it was first offered to me. Knowing I liked having it was especially important to the mother because—"

"She made it."

He was flabbergasted. "How did you know?"

"I found a shard in that cliff dwelling before I found the body. Something about the design made me uncomfortable. I didn't figure out what it was until I made a pot based on that shard. When I placed the new pot in the shop, I noted how different it was from the one you sold me. They could not both have been from the same tribe. Then I examined the one you brought. The pieces fit together like two pieces of a jigsaw puzzle."

"Why shouldn't they? They were from the same pot."

I shook my head. "Prehistoric pots were not made on wheels with processed clay. There are always irregularities and little bubbles. When they break, small pieces fall off along the fissure. Only a new pot can receive a clean break."

He laughed. "It was foolish of me to try to fool an expert, but it worked at first. I had to break the pot so it could pass as ancient. But to get back to your original question, I gave the money to the woman for her son's college fund."

"She is talented," I said. "If she has another pot as good as that one, she can add to that fund by selling it to me."

If I ever get enough money to start buying pots again, I thought to myself.

"I will make that known to her."

We looked at each other for a few seconds. I can't be sure how he felt, but I sensed a bond between us.

I rose to go. He stepped into the aisle so that I could pass. We shook hands. I started towards the door.

After a few steps, I turned back and asked, "Surely you don't own a car?"

He was puzzled briefly then laughed. "Oh, the drivers license I showed you. I got that on my sixteenth birthday at the DMV office in Hatch. I'm not sure I actually knew how to drive. But it's a small farming community. You have to have a car to get to the fields, so they were pretty lax. I renew it every five years in case I ever need a form of identification."

"You miss Hatch?"

"I miss the smell of fresh green chile roasting."

"*Vaya con Dios*," I said.

He extended his hand and made the sign of the cross. "God be with you."

# 37

*El Bastardo* was waiting for me when I stepped outside the church.

Before I could turn to grab the heavy door, his hand shot in my direction. But it was open.

"I just wanted to say goodbye."

I accepted his handshake warily.

"I was already drunk when I heard you were with Sirena. I don't even remember the fight, but she said you beat me fair and square, so no hard feelings, *que no?*"

"No hard feelings," I agreed. "I admire you for taking it like a man."

The smile on his face revealed how much he liked the compliment.

"Sirena, she also told me you two were just chaperones and not really on a date. She says I have to think before I get mad. I know she is right, but I'm not too good at thinking."

He looked me up and down. "Even with me drunk, I can't

believe a little shrimp wearing a cast could knock me out. You must be one tough *vato*."

"*Las apariencias engañan*," I said, certain that he didn't get the double entendre of my appearance being deceiving and him being deceived about what knocked him out.

When I reached the truck, Susannah said, "Jeez, Hubie, you must have been a very bad boy. You were in confession almost an hour."

I fastened my seatbelt and she started out of the *placita*.

"Actually," I said, "I was in confession for only a couple of minutes. I spent the rest of the time sitting on a pew talking to Alvar Nuñez."

She almost rammed one of the deserted storefronts. "Nuñez was in the church? So everyone here *was* lying to protect him."

"No. They just don't know his name."

"Impossible. Everyone knows everyone here."

"Everyone does know him. They just don't know him as Alvar Nuñez. They know him as Father Jerome."

This time she barely missed the gas station, possibly saving us from death and the village from a fiery end by stopping just inches from the one pump. If you want premium in La Reina, you're out of luck.

"Alvar Nuñez is the local priest? I can hardly believe it."

"I saw him when he came out of the office to take your confession."

"But you saw his drivers license that said Alvar Nuñez."

"That's the name his parents gave him and the one he had when he was sixteen and got his license. But when he became a Dominican, he took a new name."

She turned off the engine and rolled down the windows. The air at 8,000 feet was cool and fresh. "Did you find out why he lured you to the cliff dwelling?"

I had almost forgotten that was the purpose of our visit. So much had happened, but none of it seemed to mean anything. I told her what Father Jerome told me.

"So did Father Groaz change his name?" she asked.

I explained what I had learned about the distinction between a diocesan priest and a priest who is a brother in one of the orders like the Dominicans, the Franciscans or the Jesuits.

"I guess I don't know much about my own church," she said.

"At least you know about confession. If you hadn't decided to make one, I wouldn't have seen Alvar . . . er, Father Jerome."

"So what? Nothing came of it. This whole thing has been one giant goose chase. If you had a cell phone, none of this would have happened. You could have called me from that cliff dwelling. I would have come to get you. You wouldn't have trekked across the wilderness with a wounded coyote and a dog. You wouldn't have sprained your ankle. Maybe you would even have listened to reason and reported the body to the police. They could have found it before it was moved and figured out who murdered it."

"I don't think a cell phone could get a signal there."

"And your kiln won't work without electricity."

"Huh?"

"You have a kiln even though there are times you can't use it, just like a cell phone. Even murder mystery fans understand that."

"Murder mystery fans?" Susannah weaves her own logic, but I can't fault her. She usually figures things out before I do.

"Yeah. They have a website called DorothyL, and they've been talking about how irritating it is when an author uses 'no cell phone' as an excuse."

Now I was really confused. "As an excuse for what?"

"For something in a mystery like a detective not calling for back-up, or a person not calling his best friend when he discovers a body in a cliff dwelling."

"And who is Dorothielle? The name sounds like she could be Miss Gladys' sister."

"It's not a name, Hubert. It's a first name and a middle initial, Dorothy L. As in Sayers, the famous murder mystery writer."

Now it was beginning to make sense. The reason she was upset had nothing to do with my not having a cell phone, although she does complain about that. What was irritating her was that the murder mystery she thought we could solve had turned out not to be a murder.

She steered back on to the road.

"I wouldn't say nothing came of it," I said. "I know the body was a modern person. I know Father Jerome tricked me into going out there hoping I would find the body and report it. And I know I should have taken your advice and reported it the first time you mentioned it."

She was tactful enough not to say she told me so. What she did say was, "You still don't know the important stuff. Who stole your Bronco? Who was the dead guy?"

"Yeah, and what happened to my hat?"

"It blew away. Forget it."

"Consider it forgotten. I do agree that the identity of the dead guy is puzzling. A dilemma in fact."

"Exactly. If the dead guy was from La Reina, why aren't they worried about him? Looking for him? And if he *wasn't* from La Reina, why was he in the ceremony?"

I shrugged. "Not my problem."

"I still think he was murdered."

"The hole in his hand was made by a nail, Suze, not a bullet. He volunteered to play Jesus in a reenactment of the Crucifixion."

She shuddered. "Why would anyone do that?"

"They believe they must suffer for their sins."

"They claim to be Christians," she said, "but they don't seem to get the message. Jesus suffered for us. We don't need to repeat his ordeal."

"People have been doing it for almost a thousand years. I think the *Flagellantes* started in Italy around the year 1200."

"You remember that scary guy in *The Da Vinci Code* who whipped his back until it looked like hamburger?"

"Silas," I said.

"There really are people like him," she said, the idea obviously hard for her to accept.

We drove along in silence until we reached the paved road.

"Well, Hubie, I won our wager. The dead guy was definitely modern. So you have to take my car."

"I don't want your car."

"You can't back out now. A deal is a deal. Now I can buy a new car."

"I can't drive with this cast, so you might as well keep your car for now." I was hoping to wiggle out of this deal and wanted to buy time.

"The first thing we have to do is retrieve it," she said. "There's a reception Saturday at the La Rinconada Gallery in San Patricio. The art department is sponsoring one graduate student to attend, and I was selected. So I get a guest cottage free for one night. I want you to come with me. We can stop by the ranch the second night on the way home and switch the truck back for my car."

"That's a nice offer, Suze, but I think I'd just be in your way."

"You wouldn't be in my way. You'd be good company. I don't want to drive all the way down there by myself. And you need to get away. This Rio Doloroso thing has been tough on you."

"I don't—"

"Listen, Hubert. I drove you all the way to that cliff dwelling so you could go down there to find pots and check the age of a dead guy, neither of which you did. Then I drove you all the way up here to La Reina where you got into a bar fight, and I got accused of being a witch. The least you can do is ride along with me to La Rinconada."

I smiled at her. "When do we leave?"

"Tomorrow afternoon."

"Good. I was planning to sleep late."

# 38

Our route to San Patricio took us through Willard—population 249.

Then we started hitting the *really* small towns: Progresso, Cedarvale, Corona and Robshart—population 18, but I suspect they are counting the cemetery.

As we entered Carrizozo, population 996 and the current county seat of Lincoln County, I reminded Susannah of the local ordinance that prohibits women from appearing in public unshaven.

"I have no plan to stop," she said, "but I shaved my legs this morning in case the engine blows up and I have to get out of the truck and appear in public."

I was laughing when she added, "I also wore clean underwear in case we're in an accident. Mom would be proud of me."

*Carizzo* is the Spanish word for reed and *carizzozo* is the adjectival form, 'reedy'. Reeds don't grow in deserts, so I assume the Spanish named the town for the wiry grass that grows in the surrounding plains. Or maybe they were referring to some women with coarse leg hair that they didn't want to encounter in public on the *paseo*.

We turned east on U.S. 380. Since we were getting closer, Susannah told me about La Rinconada. It features paintings by Peter Hurd, Henriette Wyeth-Hurd, Michael Hurd, Andrew Wyeth and N.C. Wyeth. I gathered the Wyeths and Hurds are all in-laws, and one or more of them own the gallery.

"The only painting I know by any of that bunch is Andrew Wyeth's *Cristina's World*," I said.

"You won't get to see that one. It's in the Museum of Modern Art in New York. You like it?"

"There's something about the girl in the picture that makes me want to know her story."

"Everyone feels that way, Hubie. That's why it's such a famous piece. It captivates viewers. Wyeth was inspired to paint it when he saw a neighbor named Christina Olson crawling across a field. She couldn't walk because she suffered from Charcot-Marie-Tooth disease."

"A tooth disease can prevent someone from walking?"

"It's not a tooth disease. Charcot, Marie and Tooth were the names of the three people who discovered the disease. The figure in the painting is actually Wyeth's wife Betsy who posed for the painting."

"Then why isn't it called *Betsy's World*?"

"Because it was Christina who inspired the painting. Betsy was just the model."

"What about the house at the top of the hill she's looking up at? Is it one of those Hollywood sets that's just a flat surface with the front of a house painted on it?"

I was feeling disillusioned.

"No, Wyeth painted from the real house. It's called the Olson House."

"So he used the real house but a fake person."

"Betsy Wyeth was not a fake person."

"You know what I mean. It's supposed to be a painting of Christina Olson looking longingly up the hill to her house where they're serving tea and scones or something, and she's sad because it seems so far away and she can't walk because she's got a sore tooth. And up until a moment ago, my appreciation of the painting was even greater because I now know what it's like to be mobility impaired. But even though that's the way the house really looked, the woman in the picture got up and walked away after Wythe finished painting, and that spoils the painting for me."

Susannah was laughing now. "If Christina had been in the painting and you found out about her, that would have spoiled it for you, too."

"How so?"

"Because Christina Olson refused to use a wheelchair. She said she didn't want to be beholden to anyone. As a result, she lived in squalor."

"No wonder people don't understand modern art," I said, and she laughed even harder.

We passed through Capitan and Lincoln before backtracking on U.S. 70 for three miles to San Patricio. We had traveled two hundred miles through eleven villages with a combined population smaller than a freshman history course at the University of New Mexico.

The La Rinconada Gallery is part of the Sentinel Ranch which has a scattering of private residences and a few guest cottages. It struck me as a perfect combination of urban sophistication and pastoral relaxation, Virginia Woolf meets Dale Evans.

The ranch is cradled in quiet rolling hills along the Rio Ruidoso, 'noisy river' in Spanish. But think of noisy as water flowing over rocks in a Japanese garden, not noisy as in Niagara Falls.

We checked into the Apple House, a modest pink adobe with a tin roof. The cottonwood, aspens and Lombardy poplars had just begun to turn. The yellows and golds were magnificent against the pink walls.

We had just enough time to change, refresh and head for the reception.

We were greeted at the entrance by an elderly Hispanic gentleman holding a tray of champagne flutes. Bubbles rose from a strawberry at the bottom of each glass. I was reaching for a glass to determine if it might be Gruet when a man with an in-charge countenance took the tray from the older gentleman.

"I'll greet the guests," he said. "Go fill some glasses. And put on a tie."

The older gentleman nodded, said, "Yes, sir," and left.

The man now holding the tray moved it out of my reach and said, "I'm sorry sir, but we cannot allow you to enter with a foot cast. Our cherry wood floors are quite delicate. They were milled from local trees and we are fastidious about them because . . . well, we can hardly go to Home Depot and buy a replacement piece if one is damaged, can we?" He laughed his authoritative laugh. "We can, however, offer you the use of one of our wheelchairs with soft rubber tires."

"That's very kind," I said, "but out of respect for Christina Olson, I never use a wheelchair."

He took a step back and gave me an uncertain smile.

I gestured to Susannah and said, "Ms. Inchaustigui is an art historian. I am simply her driver. I would enjoy a stroll around the trees."

There was visible relief on his face. The sunburned guy with the skinned nose and cast was not going to embarrass the other guests with their spa-smooth faces and their hedge-fund plump wallets.

"Please do not hesitate to let me know if you change your mind," he said with a smile. You could have lubricated an eighteen-wheeler with the oil in his voice.

I started down to the river using my crutches.

I was just to the back of the main building when I heard someone call out, *Señor.*

I turned to see the gentleman who had initially been serving the champagne.

"I am sorry you were not allowed to enter. I am in the kitchen filling glasses. Can I bring you something? We have the champagne you saw. We also have many kinds of fine liquors."

"What would you have if you were going to relax over by those trees?" I asked him.

There was a mixture of merriment and mischief in his eyes. "There is some expensive whiskey."

"I'll go in with you and fix myself a glass of it."

He smiled. "No, *Señor.* I do not wish to have the marks from your cast on the fine linoleum in the kitchen. I will bring it to you."

He returned moments later with a quart of High West Rocky Mountain Rye 21 Year Old Whiskey.

"I brought two glasses in case your *patrona* decides to join you," he said and winked.

I thanked him profusely even though I had never heard of the brand, and rye sounded like a close cousin of pumpernickel, the taste of which had clung to my taste buds like hot on a jalapeño.

There were a few outbuildings and a barn closer to the river. I sat down on a weathered wood bench in front of a fire pit.

I was content to listen to the rippling water and breathe in the fresh air. After a while, I heard footsteps and turned.

He seemed to materialize out of the glooming, a figure backlit by the sun dropping below the Sacramento Mountains. He stepped to me and offered his hand.

"Howdy. Jack Truesdell," he said, "but folks call me Cactus."

His hand was one continuous callus and felt way too tough to drive a rebar through.

"Pleased to meet you. I'm Hubert Schuze."

"I was just stepping out for a smoke. You don't mind, do you?"

"No," I lied.

He popped the snap on his shirt pocket, pulled out a bag of tobacco and did something I'd never seen before except in old movies. He rolled a cigarette. After he stuck it in his mouth, I half expected him to produce a wooden match and ignite it with a flick of his thumbnail.

He did use a match, but he ignited it by drawing it across his right boot. The hand-rolled paper flared, casting a brief light on a face with a thousand stories etched upon it.

From his scuffed riding boots to his sweat-stained cowboy hat, he looked like a character from a spaghetti western. His frame was scrawny and twisted, his face lean and angular. Scars, bumps and missing teeth indicated a life of rough rides over rocky trails.

"How did you get the nickname Cactus?"

"Spent most of my life prospecting in the Mogollons. Folks started calling me Cactus cause they knowed I had to be tough as a cactus to survive up there."

"Where did you live?"

"Mostly in the mines I was workin'. A man's got to dig into the side of the mountain to find ore up there. There ain't much flat ground. After you done all that digging, you got a place out of the weather even if you don't strike nuthin."

"Sounds like a tough life."

He shook his head and took a long drag from his smoke. "Best life there is. My daddy worked all his life in the Little Fannie Mine. They let him go because of the panic of 1930. His first wife was washed away in the flood of '23. He married my mother a few years later, so he had a young wife and a new young'un to support but didn't have two dimes to rub together. He took the family back to Silver City where he'd growed up. I didn't take to city life. So when I hit sixteen, I bought a burro and headed into the mountains. But I never worked for no mining company cause I saw how they treated my daddy."

Cactus struck another match and lit the kindling in the fire pit.

"Gets chilly when the sun goes down," he said. "You got any whiskey?"

He must have been watching all along.

I handed him a glass and poured us each some rye.

After our first sips—his was actually more of a guzzle—I asked him when he had stopped prospecting.

"It was near ten years ago. I'd just sold some silver and was fixin' to buy supplies when a fella in the feed store overheard the clerk call my name. He asked if I was kin to the Jack Truesdell went to school with Billy the Kid, and I told him that was my daddy."

"Your father went to school with Billy the Kid?"

"Yep. That's what got me this here job. That fella was from these parts. He told me I could have a job at the museum in Lincoln tellin' folks about Billy the Kid. I was nearin' seventy, and getting up and down that mountain weren't getting' no easier, so I throwed my knapsack in his truck and moved to Lincoln."

207

He held out his glass, and I gave him a refill. I gave myself one too so as not to lose ground. After all, it was my bottle.

He laughed. "I didn't last long. You can tell I'm a fella likes to talk. But they wanted me to stick to stuff they wrote down. I told 'em I don't read too good, and they said I could just memorize it. But my memory was worse than my readin', so I quit before they could fire me and took a job here mowin' the fields, pickin' up the trash the tourists throw out and keepin' the tack room nice and tidy."

"How could your father have gone to school with Billy the Kid? That was ages ago."

"Daddy was born a year or two after Billy. When he was twelve, Silver City got its first school, and the two of them started together. I growed up on the stories daddy told me about him and Billy. They was best friends. Seven years later, Billy was dead. Daddy lived to be over eighty just like me. Us Truesdells are a hardy bunch. He always wondered how things might'a worked out if Billy hadn't been double-crossed by General Wallace."

I remembered the publisher's introduction to *Ben-Hur* claimed Wallace wrote the final scenes after returning from a clandestine meeting with Billy the Kid.

So I asked Cactus about the double cross. He told me what his father had told him and recommended I drop by the museum to learn more. By the time he had completed the story, the bottle was half empty.

He tossed another dry log on the fire. "I can't take the cold like I used to. My hands is cold. My ears is cold. Even this here scar is cold," he said, pointing to a disfigured patch on his right cheek. "I guess no blood can get there."

"How'd that happen?"

He laughed. "Done it to myself. I was working a claim on the east side of Bearwallow Mountain when one of my back tooths started hurting something fierce. I tried to prize it out with my jack-knife, but it wouldn't budge. The pain got so bad, I tried to knock it out with my little rock hammer, but I couldn't get a good swing at it. I decided to just wait it out. But after two days, I couldn't take no more. I carried a little .22 pistol in those day to fight off varmints and claim jumpers. So I decided to blow the tooth out."

"You shot your tooth!"

He gave a quick nod. "First I prized off a slug and dumped out half the powder from the casing. I carved the slug down so it was smaller and more pointy. Then I put it back on the casing. I put the muzzle at the bottom of the tooth and aimed up a bit. I guess it hurt, but the toothache was so bad, I hardly noticed it. I took a swig of whiskey and rolled it around. I hated to waste the whisky, but I figured I didn't need blood and tooth pieces in my gut, so I spit it out. Course I'd had a few swallers before shooting the tooth just to steady my aim. A flap of meat and skin was hanging off the hole in my cheek. I swabbed it with bacon grease and pushed it back in place. Then I tied my bandanna around my head and went to sleep."

"How could you sleep after that?"

"I hadn't slept for two nights. Once that tooth stopped throbbing like a bull's heart, I dropped right off. The next morning my mouth tasted like I'd ate a coyote, but the hole was already beginning to scab. A week later it was right as rain."

It was dark now and the fire cast shifting shadows on his face. "That's an awfully big scar for just a .22." I said.

"It might have been infested," he said. "It bled off and on for days."

"You said it scabbed over and healed in a week."

He removed his hat and scratched his head. There were a few patches of grey stubble, a dent the size of a tablespoon and a long jagged scar.

He put the hat back on. "Guess my memory ain't so good these days." He held his glass between the fire and his eyes. "This shore is good whiskey. Lot better'n that stuff I had up on the mountain."

# 39

Truesdell left around eleven. I walked back to the Apple House and found Susannah had left the door unlocked for me.

People who live in big cities may find that scary, but it didn't strike me as strange. I live in a big city, part of which is dangerous, I'm sorry to say. But even in Albuquerque there's an understanding of what the rest of the state is like. Villages where people go out at three in the morning to open and close gates in *acequias*. Places where there are no bad neighborhoods because there are no neighborhoods at all. There is only the village.

The people are not better or worse than city people. There are just too few of them for things to go too far wrong. They live in a different setting. If *El Bastardo* lived in certain neighborhoods in Albuquerque, there would be others like him. If he was bested in a bar fight, they would urge him to get even. Offer to help. That's how gangs start.

But in La Reina, he extends his hand and says "no hard feelings." People in villages may not always like each other, but they almost always coexist peaceably.

Thanks to the best whiskey I ever drank, I slept soundly on the couch. Okay, it may have been the quantity of whiskey rather than the quality that aided my sleep, but I felt refreshed in the morning.

We drove to Lincoln and had breakfast at The Wortley Hotel, actual motto: No Guests Gunned Down in Over 100 Years.

Lincoln was the county seat of the largest county in the United States until other counties were carved out of it. The town faded into obscurity and was replaced as county seat by Carrizozo. The historical buildings were eventually taken over by the state as a museum. Because Lincoln had the courthouse, jail, sheriff's office and saloons in its heyday, it was also the place where many episodes of the Lincoln County War played out, including Billy the Kid's most famous jail break.

I asked our waiter about it, and he was happy to oblige. Because Lincoln is now more a museum than a town, everyone there is a tourist guide either formally or informally.

He pointed across the street.

"Billy was over there wearing shackles and waiting to be hanged. Marshall Bob Olinger was sitting at this very table. Billy was being guarded by Deputy James Bell. Billy asked Bell to take him to the outhouse behind the courthouse. When they got back inside the courthouse, a pistol shot was heard. Bell ran out of the courthouse and fell dead from a bullet wound."

Susannah said, "I'll bet someone hid a pistol in the outhouse so Billy could get it."

"Yep, that's what most people figure. Billy then gets Olinger's shotgun from the armory and positions himself by that window," he says, again pointing across the street.

"Olinger jumped up from this table when he heard the shot and charged outside. 'Did Bell kill the Kid?' he yelled out. A man named Godfrey Gauss replied, 'No, The Kid has killed Bell.'

Billy called out from the window, 'Hello Bob'. Olinger sees the shotgun and replies to Gauss, 'Yes, and he's killed me too'. Which Billy does by blasting him with both barrels."

Susannah shuddered.

"How could he do all that in shackles?" I asked.

"He was famous for having thin wrists. He slipped the shackles off with ease."

"Olinger and Bell must not have known that," said Susannah. "It was smart of Billy to leave the shackles on until he was ready to make his move. Gave them a false sense of security."

Our waiter told us Billy threw the shotgun through the window onto Olinger's body then went back to the armory for a Winchester rifle, two pistols and two cartridge belts loaded with ammunition.

"Quite a crowd had gathered by that point. Billy talked to them from the balcony, telling them he hadn't planned to kill Bell. He was just going to lock him in the cell. But Bell ran, so Billy said he was left with no choice. He also told them he didn't want to kill anyone else, but he would if anyone tried to interfere with his escape. The manager of this hotel grabbed a gun to stop the escape but was restrained by two friends with cooler heads. If our manager tried to do that today, no one on the staff would lift a finger," he said with a scowl.

"That's awful," Susannah said.

He gave us a big smile. "Just kidding. We all love Vic and Cathy."

"So he got away?" I asked.

"Yeah, he took a horse belonging to Billy Burt, the county clerk. He said to the crowd, 'Tell Billy Burt I'll send his pony back, and don't look for me this side of Ireland. *Adios*, boys'. And he rode out of town singing."

We walked across to the courthouse museum and paid the five dollar admission fee. Susannah studied the various old artifacts while I read the letters exchanged between Lew Wallace and Billy the Kid.

One from Billy dated March 4, 1881 read as follows:

To Gov. Lew Wallace

Dear Sir

I wrote you a little note the day before yesterday but have received no answer. I expect you have forgotten what you promised me, this month two years ago, but I have not and I think you had ought to have come and seen me as I requested you to. I have done everything that I promised you I would and you have done nothing that you promised me.

I think when you think the matter over, you will come down and see me, and I can then explain everything to you.

Judge Leonard passed through here on his way east in January and promised to come and see me on his way back, but he did not fulfill his promise. It looks to me like I am getting left in the cold. I am not treated right by Sherman. He lets Every Stranger that comes to see me through Curiosity in to see me, but will not let a Single one of my friends in, not even an Attorney.

I guess they mean to send me up without giving me any Show but they will have a nice time doing it. I am not entirely without friends.

I shall expect to see you some time today.

Patiently Waiting, I am truly Yours Respectfully.

Wm. H. Bonney

Another one started:

Sir, I will keep the appointment I made but be sure and have men come that you can depend on. I am not afraid to die like a man fighting but I would not like to be killed like a dog unarmed.

I was struck by the simple prose of this young man who had only two years of formal schooling. In my opinion, both his writing and his behavior were more forthright than Lew Wallace.

# 40

We left Lincoln and headed west on U.S 70. About halfway through the Mescalero Apache Reservation we turned left on NM 244 up to Cloudcroft. My parents used to rent a cabin there in the summer when it was too hot in Albuquerque. At almost 9,000 feet, it's never hot in Cloudcroft.

I told Susannah about my conversation with Cactus Truesdell.

She was giving me one of those looks. "You are so gullible. To begin with, there is no way his father went to school with Billy the Kid. Billy died in the nineteenth century."

"It was *late* in the nineteenth century. Cactus is over eighty. His father was also over eighty when he died. So the two of them stretch back 160 years."

"Only if he fathered Cactus on his death bed. And even then he wouldn't have been able to tell his son all those stories because he would be dead."

"Okay, say he was seventy when Cactus was born. I remember

lots of things my father told me when I was ten, some of them on this very road on our way to a cabin."

"A seventy-year-old couple conceived a child?"

"Cactus' mother was his father's second wife. She was a lot younger. The first wife was washed away in a flood."

"Likely story," she said. "The dirty old man probably threw her in the river because he had his eye on a younger woman."

"If Cactus was conceived when his father was seventy," I said, "that still reaches back to the right era."

"Right, an era when mountain men practiced dentistry with pistols. Face it, Hubie, that old coot was pulling your leg so hard, it's a wonder you're not six feet tall this morning."

"It doesn't matter if everything he told me was made from whole cloth spun from imaginary thread. The important thing is he gave me a possible solution to the dilemma."

"The dilemma about the identity of the dead guy? That if he was from La Reina, why aren't they worried about him? And if he *wasn't* from La Reina, why was he in the ceremony? That dilemma? Because that one's easy." She laughed. "All we have to do is find someone who is and is not from La Reina."

"Exactly," I said.

"Exactly?"

"Exactly. You know why Billy the Kid was in jail awaiting hanging?"

"This is just a wild guess, Hubert, but maybe it was because he had murdered someone."

"No, I don't mean what *crime* got him in jail. I mean how did they manage to get him in jail."

"I wondered about that. He was the most feared gunman in the West. He was fast on the draw, a deadly accurate shot and had nerves of steel. Plus he also had a lot of friends who would protect him. I don't think there was a lawman alive who could've captured him."

"Right. And no one did capture him. He turned himself in."

"Why would he do that?"

"Because the Territorial Governor had promised him immunity."

"Lew Wallace?"

I nodded.

"If he had immunity, why were they planning to hang him?"

"Because Wallace withdrew the immunity."

"He double-crossed him?"

"He did. And when I started thinking about that—"

"Wait, don't tell me."

NM 244 is the back road between Cloudcroft and Ruidoso, the two major resort towns in the Sacramento mountains. It winds its way through grassy valleys between hillsides of pine and aspen.

The truck's big V-8 engine pulled us up the slopes effortlessly, its hum the only sound. The turning aspen leaves fluttered in a gentle breeze.

"I've got it," she said. "The dead guy was from La Reina. But he had left for some reason. He was lured back. Maybe not with a promise of immunity, but with something that convinced him to return just like the immunity convinced Billy to turn himself in."

"Exactly. Nothing else makes sense."

"So we have two things to figure out," she said, sliding comfortably into her Nancy Drew persona. "First, why did he flee? Second, what lured him back?"

"When Whit reported back to me after talking to his police contacts in that part of the state, he said the people they have on their missing list are people they suspect have relocated of their own volition, people running out on child support or skipping bail, things like that."

"Did he get their names?"

"I don't think so. At that point, I thought what we were looking for was someone who had disappeared for no evident reason."

"But he could call them back and get the names, right?"

"I assume so. I'll call him when we get back."

She reached into her purse on the seat between us and fished out her cell phone.

"Why not call him now?" she said and handed me the phone.

I did, and he agreed to check and get back to me. The people who read DorothyL would be proud of me.

Susannah wanted to buy a present for her father's upcoming birthday, so she headed for the quirky gift shops in the little village.

I spotted a sign for Imaginary Books. Cloudcroft being a small village, I figured it was probably a place where you could order one of those electronic books Tristan reads. With no paper or ink, 'imaginary' is a good word for them. But the little second floor shop above the bank and next to the local newspaper, *The Mountain Monthly*, had real books.

Ed the proprietor sold me two books, *The Saga of Billy the Kid* by Walter Noble Burns and *The Authentic Life of Billy the Kid* by Pat F. Garrett.

There's a short order station at the back of the Mountaintop Mercantile. The friendly teenager working there fixed us two green chile burritos to go, and I bought one of their fresh-baked apple pies to take to the Inchaustiguis.

We came down the mountain and stopped to buy pistachios at

McGinn's Pistachio Tree Ranch. It felt like we were on vacation, and we were making the most of it. Besides, pistachios are great with Gruet. Susannah took a picture of me standing under the 25-foot high pistachio made of plaster, insisting that I position myself so that the nut seemed to be growing out of my head.

The girl has a wacky sense of humor.

# 41

The rambunctious dog that greeted us on our last visit intercepted us a half mile from the house. Susannah stopped, and he leapt into the bed of the truck where he ran from side to side as we approached the house, protecting us from varmints both left and right.

The entire Inchaustigui family was on the porch.

"Hi, Mr. Inchaustigui," I said.

"Looks like we'll be seeing a lot of each other, Hubie, so you might as well start calling me Gus."

I swallowed hard and shook his hand.

After all the handshakes and hugs, Susannah and her parents went inside. Mark and Matt stayed on the porch with me.

"We'll give you a hand with the luggage," Matt said.

As we headed back to the truck, Mark said. "We've put you two in the front guestroom. We're sort of old-fashioned, but after our little talk, we decided it's okay if you two bunk together."

"Oh," I said quickly, "we don't do that."

Smiles of relief spread across their faces.

"I guess you're old-fashioned yourself," said Matt. "That's great to hear."

"I knew we were right about you," added Mark, patting me on the shoulder, "You're a straight shooter, Hubie."

I felt like a complete phony as I trailed behind them up onto the porch and into the house. If I were really a straight shooter, I would have set the record straight right then and there. But I couldn't. I know it makes little sense, but I thought I'd be stepping on Susannah's toes and hurting her feelings if I disavowed any romance between us. It was her family. I had to discuss it with her first and trust her to handle it correctly.

Matt and Mark carried the two suitcases. I carried the pie. Given the way they had looked at it, I knew it would never see the morrow.

I got the front guestroom. Susannah got the room she grew up in. After we'd washed off the road dust, we gathered in the living room. Matt and Mark had beer, Susannah and Hilary had wine. Gus and I had whiskey over ice.

It wasn't as good as High West Rocky Mountain Rye 21 Year Old, but it also didn't cost $130 a bottle, which is what I later discovered to be the price of High West.

I told him it was good whiskey and asked what brand it was. He handed me the bottle of Don Quixote Blue Corn Bourbon. Made in New Mexico, obviously. Where else would they make bourbon from blue corn?

I love blue corn, and it doesn't bother me that the dishes I make with it are blue. That just shows they have that good juju that's in blueberries and other wonder foods. Personally, I pay little attention to that stuff. I just eat what's fresh and tastes good.

But I have to say I was glad the whiskey was not blue.

What I was not glad about was Gus hoisting his glass and saying, "A toast—to Hubie and Susannah."

After a second round of drinks with a lot of reminiscing and banter among the Inchaustiguis, we made our way to the dining room where a table sagged under the weight of a bowl of salad, a plate of fresh-baked bread, a bowl of redskinned potatoes, a platter of roasted ears of corn, a big bowl of thick dark gravy and a roast that must have weighed fifteen pounds.

The roast was narrow on the end where a bone protruded and basketball-sized at the other end. It looked like a drumstick from a pterodactyl, which would be a good Scrabble word if you ever faced a situation where you needed one that starts with 'pt'.

The bowls were passed around family-style. I gave myself diet-sized helpings of potatoes and salad and one ear of corn. I passed on the bread.

Then Gus asked me to hand him my plate because he was carving.

"I see you left a lot of room on your plate for the lamb," he said and sawed off a caveman portion.

I've never liked gravy, but when the gravy boat left my hand, it had been reduced from a boat to a small canoe. The consistency was standard for gravy, which is to say it had the mouthfeel of warm glue. But the taste was okay—herbs, garlic and something pungent like Worcestershire.

I cut a tidbit of lamb and dredged it through the gravy. The texture was like beef, but there was an odd taste, like beef from a steer with a hormone imbalance. I was able to finish the lamb. The gravy helped.

Susannah's smirks did not. I was beginning to suspect her hand in this menu.

The pie never had a chance. I should have bought two.

They turned in early in rancher style. Probably had to get up early to milk the sheep.

I read the Walter Noble Burns book and discovered a Billy the Kid far different from the popular legend.

# 42

Breakfast at the Inchaustigui ranch is designed to sustain the body for a long day of digging fence post holes and dragging calves out of mud bogs.

I'm not sure they actually do those things, but the eggs, bacon, sausage and biscuits had me ready to give it a try.

And I could have used the exercise. Days of sitting in a truck interrupted only by stops for high-calorie food had me struggling with the top button of my blue jeans.

The truck had taken us to Rio Doloroso where we discovered an empty grave, to La Reina where we discovered that Alvar Nuñez was Father Jerome and to Lincoln County where I discovered Cactus Truesdell.

I asked Susannah to keep it for one more trip.

"To?"

I stood there by her car but didn't say anything.

"You want to go back to that cliff dwelling," she said.

"Not to it. Just by it."

"Why?"

"Call it a hunch."

"Sounds like fun," she said.

"I've got a bone to pick with you," I said once we were on pavement and headed back to Albuquerque.

I could see the mischief in her eyes even in profile.

"Would that be a lamb bone?" she asked in her little-miss-innocent voice.

"You set me up. Me, your best friend. Do I give you margaritas made with *mixto* tequila? Do I give you salsa made with canned tomatoes? Stop laughing. It's difficult to scold you when you're laughing."

"Admit it, you liked it. You ate every bite of that huge piece."

"Only because I didn't want to offend your mom."

She was still laughing. "You ate so much lamb you couldn't even finish your potatoes or your corn. You actually liked it."

After she finally stopped laughing, I told her about the Walter Noble Burns book.

"So the locals considered Billy the Kid a hero?" she asked.

"Most of them. Especially the Hispanics."

"Why?"

"You know about the Lincoln County War, right?"

"Some. We studied it in school, and part of it took place on our land."

"Then you know the gang led by Murphy and Dolan ran Lincoln county like a fiefdom. Murphy had the only store, so any business transaction went though him. They controlled the sheriff and the court. One resident was quoted in the book as saying, 'They intimidated, oppressed, and crushed people who were obliged to deal with them'."

"And most of those people were Hispanic?"

"Right. The Dolan and Murphy gang were Johnny-come-lately gringos who basically took over the area and treated the original inhabitants, both Hispanics and Indians, as peons. Then the powerful Texas cattleman John Chisum brought a large herd up from Texas, creating competition for the Murphy faction. Murphy's lawyer, a man of principle named McSween, was fed up with Murphy's crooked ways, so he went to work for Chisum. Billy the Kid also quit the Murphy gang and went over to Chisum. And the Chisum camp was strengthened when an eccentric Englishman named John Tunstall bought a ranch in the area and allied himself with Chisum. In addition to ranching, Tunstall set up a mercantile store in competition with Murphy. The locals abandoned Murphy's store because Tunstall offered decent prices and fair dealings."

"And that's why they killed him," she said.

"Yes. They trumped up some phony charge against him and sent a posse of drunken hooligans to arrest him. They found Tunstall riding among his cattle. Tunstall saw them coming and rode over to greet them. 'Howdy, boys,' he said, and they shot him in the head. He was unarmed. In fact, he had never carried a gun in his life. Then for good measure, they used a big rock to smash in his skull, killed his horse and lined the two up together on the ground."

"How can people do things like that?"

"I have no idea. When Billy the Kid found Tunstall, he vowed to kill every man who had anything to do with the murder."

"Tunstall's murder set off the Lincoln County War," she said.

"Yes, and led to Billy the Kid's reputation as a killer. But from his point of view—and the point of view of the locals—he was just avenging a friend. It's normally wrong to take the law into your own hands, but what do you do when the law is in the hands of the bad guys?"

Susannah told me about some cattle rustled by Billy from a herd Murphy was running on a spread near Progresso that he had no right to use. The land belonged to an Hispanic family, but they dared not complain for fear of retribution. Some of Murphy's men were positioned to ambush Billy when he drove the cattle south to Lincoln. But a friend from Progresso named Ponciano Chavez alerted Billy. So he drove the cattle northwest around Jumanes Knob then south, blazing a trail through Rogers canyon and Deuson Draw that the Inchaustiguis still use today to drive their cattle and sheep to the lower ground on the south of their ranch.

I eventually worked up the nerve to broach the subject I had been dreading.

"What did you think of the toast your dad made to the two of us?"

"Typical dad. He loves to make toasts and announcements."

"When I greeted him on the porch, he said he and I were going to be seeing a lot of each other, so I should call him Gus."

"Yep. He's not one for formalities."

Hmm. Either she hadn't picked up on what I took to be her family's misinterpretation of our relationship, or I was the one who had misinterpreted. So I went to the one statement that seemed the most obvious.

"When Matt and Mark got our luggage out of the truck, Mark said, 'We've put you two in the front guestroom. We're sort of old-fashioned, but we decided it's okay if you two bunk together'."

"Sure. They know we shared a room at the Lawrence Ranch, and I told them we would both be in the Apple House down in San Patricio." She laughed. "I guess they decided you're not a threat to my honor."

This was harder than I expected.

I decided to abandon my futile effort to convince her that her family thought we were an item.

# 43

Whit Fletcher came to my shop about an hour after Susannah dropped me off.

His first words were, "You got any coffee?"

The next words out of his mouth—not counting the disparaging ones he leveled at the coffee—were 'Carlos Campos Castillo'.

"You remember that name?" he asked.

"I remember all three of them, but I can't swear that was the order they were in. I have them written down somewhere."

"It was on the list you gave me."

"If you say so. The only thing I can remember without consulting my list is that there were three individuals with a total of nine names, six of which were *apellidos*."

He frowned, whether at the word *apellidos* or at the coffee I can't say.

"I talked to the sheriff up there after your call. Turns out this Castillo is on their missing persons list, but they ain't looking for him because they think they know the reason he left town."

Whit was on the case. I got him on it by hinting there might be a valuable pot or two in the cliff dwelling. But I had gone over it with a fine-toothed rebar and knew full well there was not so much as a shard. I was worried about not being able to deliver the goods.

"Actually," I said, "you should call him Campos."

He pulled out his pocket notebook and looked at it. "Says here 'Carlos Campos Castillo', so Castillo is his last name."

It wasn't worth explaining. I asked why Carlos had left town.

"Wait 'til you hear this one. Someone had been stealing his firewood. So he carved a plug out of a piece on his woodpile, put some gunpowder in the hole and stuck the plug of wood back in the hole."

He hesitated and looked at me. "You don't seem too surprised."

"I've heard of people doing that in remote parts of the state."

"Yeah? Well this particular piece of booby-trapped wood ended up in the stove of a guy who lived in the same village. It didn't have much powder in it. I guess the idea was to discourage the thief, not to kill him. But a piece of the log shot into the guys face and left a scar. By the time he reported it, he had started growing a beard to cover it"

I thought about it. "I don't get it. Seems like the thief would be the one who would skip town because he might be arrested for stealing wood or just didn't want to stay once the whole village knew he was a thief. Why would Carlos leave?"

"It's illegal to booby-trap anything, Hubert, but I wouldn't go after him for that, and the Sheriff up there wouldn't either. A man steals from a neighbor ain't going to get much police cooperation. The problem for our boy Carlos is the guy the wood blew up on is the biggest, meanest *hombre* in town, and you wouldn't want him angry at you."

*El Bastardo*, I immediately thought. Then I remembered he didn't have a beard.

"What was his name?" I asked.

He looked down at his notebook again and said, "Alonso Castillo Maldonado."

# 44

I figured if Sharice showed up with another stem of yucca blossoms, that would mark us as a couple. Our first tradition.

Maybe we'd then choose 'our song' although I don't think people do that these days.

I had served trout and she had served fiddleheads. I didn't want to risk serving meat in case she didn't eat it. I took the bus to the co-op and bought the ingredients for my vegetarian *chiles rellenos—poblanos*, corn, summer squash, onions, fresh oregano, cilantro, jalapeños, a vanilla bean and *crema Mexicana*. I picked up some avocados and a pink grapefruit for the salad and some heavy cream for the dessert of *pastel de tres leches*.

Men are not the only one whose hearts can be reached via their stomachs, and I definitely wanted to reach Sharice's heart. And maybe a few other areas as well.

The *rellenos* are simple but time consuming. Roast and peel the poblanos. Remove the stems and seeds. Sauté the corn, squash and onions lightly—they will finish cooking in the oven. Add chopped oregano and a little *crema Mexicana* and stuff the mixture into the *poblanos*. Bake then drizzle with a sauce made with cilantro pureed in cream, cumin and the scrapings from a fresh vanilla bean. Top with bits of sweet caramelized jalapeños.

I had the *poblanos* ready for the oven and the sauce warm in a pan. The *pastel de tres leches* was on the counter. The Gruet was in the fridge. The grapefruit had been peeled, sectioned and seeded. Only the avocados remained as they had been at the store. I like to do them at the last minute.

The plain wood table had a vibrant green silk runner and plates with a red and green *chile* design I had done for the restaurant I mentioned earlier that was called first *Schnitzel* then later *Chile Schnitzel*. With those two names, failure was the only possible outcome.

She arrived in a high-neck dress of coarse-woven linen, black with geometric patterns. No jewelry at all. Her signature violet lipstick and eye shadow. The yucca stem was in one hand, a small paper bag in the other. She held them both behind my back as we kissed.

I stepped back to admire her and she twirled.

"Vera Wang?"

"Adrianna Papell."

"I've never heard of her."

She canted her head and gave me a sideways look. "You'd never heard of Vera Wang, either, had you?"

"I thought she was a local Chinese immigrant who worked as a seamstress."

She laughed and twirled again, this time into my arms, and we kissed again.

I resisted the temptation to volunteer to shed my cast.

I put the *rellenos* in the oven and opened the Gruet.

Sharice stripped the yucca blossoms into the bowl.

"Do you have any sparkling water?" she asked.

I poured Gruet into the bowl instead.

"You impetuous devil," she said.

Geronimo was making paw prints on the French doors. We joined him outside, and Sharice gave him a doggie treat from the paper bag. It had come from a bakery, not a pet store, and it disappeared before I got a good look at it. I left Geronimo with his new best friend to prepare the avocado and grapefruit drizzled with lemon juice and almond oil.

I told her about Cactus Truesdell's tooth story and asked if she thought it could be true.

"Sure. We had an instructor who used to liven up her classes with what she called 'tales from the dentistry of old'. For most of history, the dentist's only job was to pull teeth and make false ones. There was no such thing as a filling or a repair. And there were no anesthetics. The main occupational hazards were getting bitten or punched."

"So dentists also made false teeth?"

"Sometimes they made them, usually carved from ivory taken from hippopotamus teeth or elephant tusks. But sometimes they used actual human teeth."

I winced. "Ones they had pulled from a previous client?"

"No, those would be too rotten and broken. They needed undamaged teeth, so they paid grave robbers to remove teeth from corpses."

"Jeez. And I thought contemporary grave robbers were bad. At least they don't sell parts. Or maybe they do. Should we change the subject?"

She nodded and then asked what else I had learned down south. We discussed the Lincoln County War at length because, being Canadian, she knew nothing about it other than the names of two of the principals, Billy the Kid and John Chisum.

"I've heard of the Chisum Trail all my life," she said.

"There are two of them," I said, "one named after a Chisholm spelled C-h-i-s-h-o-l-m and one after John Chisum, who was a fascinating character."

"How so?"

"He was in Texas during the Civil War so he was allied with the Confederacy. But he freed all his slaves."

"He had to after the war."

"He did it on the day the war began. Including one he bought from someone passing through on the way to California because he didn't like the way her owner was treating her. He sold beef to the Confederacy for feeding the rebel soldiers but kept the Confederate money just long enough to buy more cattle. So he didn't suffer financial ruin when the war ended because his wealth was in cattle instead of Confederate money."

"It sounds like he knew the Confederacy was going to lose right from the beginning. Do his descendants still live in Lincoln County?"

I smiled at her. "If I didn't know you were from Canada, I might think you were one of them. He was a handsome man with a delicate small mouth like yours."

She laughed. "I suspect his descendants don't have my coloring."

"You're probably right. He had brown eyes, and yours are a dazzling green."

"I meant my skin color."

"I suspect all his descendants have your skin color."

She paused in thought. "His only children came from the slave women he owned?"

"They came from his wife. He married the slave he bought from the person going to California. Her name was Jensie. They had two daughters, so none of his descendants are named Chisum."

We turned to light chitchat over desert until she said, "Where do you see this going."

"Well, I'm thinking maybe a second slice of *pastel de tres leches* and another glass of Gruet."

She gave me an indulgent smile. "I meant us, Hubie."

"I like us," I said.

"We haven't been tested," she said.

"Do we need a blood test? I didn't think they did that anymore."

She laughed. "I like your sense of humor and your iconoclastic attitude, but . . ."

"But what?"

"This is our third date, and we haven't been out in public."

I pointed down to my cast. "When this thing is off, I plan to show you off all over town."

"Some people may not like that."

"I understand that. With all the paranoid feelings about immigrants, some people may object to my dating a Canadian, but I say to them in the lingo of your national sport, go puck yourself."

"You know that's not what I meant."

I nodded.

"But you're not going to acknowledge it."

"It doesn't deserve acknowledging."

"I like you a lot, Hubert Schuze."

"And I like you a lot, Sharice Clarke."

The silk runner was not big enough to cover a Scrabble board, so I cleared the table and brought the board out. She was trouncing me as easily as she did at her house, but I had hope. There was a 't' in a long vertical word, and I had a 'p' to put immediately to its left and an 'o' and a 'y' and some of the other letters required for 'pterodactyl'. But I never got all the letters I needed. What I did manage to do was spell 'ptomaine'.

It was a pyrrhic victory.

# 45

"So Carlos Campos Castillo skipped town to avoid the wrath of Alonso Castillo Maldonado."

"Either that," I said, "or Hector Campos Gomez skipped town to avoid the wrath of Jesus Zaragosa Padilla."

"Don't confuse me," Susannah said. "I'm going to call Carlos Campos Castillo 'The Dead Guy' and Alonso Castillo Maldonado 'The Hunting Guide'."

"We don't know that Carlos Campos is The Dead Guy."

"Maybe not, but he's the leading candidate. He provides just what we needed to solve the dilemma."

"Yeah," I said, "someone who's from La Reina which explains why he could have participated with the local Penitentes. And he had already left town for another reason which explains why no one is looking for him."

I thought about that for a minute then said, "But the reason he left was because he was afraid The Hunting Guide was going to take revenge on him for the exploding firewood. Given that, why would he come back?"

"It's obvious, Hubie. The Hunting Guide must have promised The Dead Guy he wouldn't harm him, sort of given him amnesty."

"Why would The Hunting Guide do that? I met him, remember? He doesn't look like the sort of guy who forgives and forgets. And the local sheriff described him as the meanest *hombre* in town. So The Dead Guy must have given The Hunting Guide money, the deed to some property, water rights or something. There had to be a *quid pro quo*."

Her shoulders twitched. "Don't use that awful phrase. Every time I hear it, I picture Anthony Hopkins as Hannibal Lector."

"Okay, I'll just say they struck a deal. But what was it?"

"Easy. The Hunting Guide promised not to take revenge. And The Dead Guy promised to re-enact the Crucifixion."

"Being crucified is a pretty drastic thing to do just to get The Hunting Guide's forgiveness."

"Not if The Dead Guy was already one of the Penitentes, a member in good standing, so to speak. Maybe he genuinely wanted forgiveness, not just from The Hunting Guide, but from God for all his sins."

I had to admit her theory made sense. But that's all it was—a theory. There was not a single fact to back it up.

I had the topo map in my lap, but didn't really need it. By this point, I knew every dune and boulder by both their Christian names and their *apellidos*.

We reached the spot from which I had twice been lowered over the cliff. From there, the course I had taken on foot that ended when I fell and sprained my ankle was chosen because it was a straight line to La Reina. A straight line may be the shortest, but it isn't necessarily drivable. I had walked between boulders and some sturdy junipers.

So I had to start navigating again at that point because Susannah had to find ground suitable for the truck. I had my head turned looking at Cerro Roto with a protractor in my hand to make a better estimate of the angle when she slammed on the brakes and yelled, "I don't believe it!"

I turned in my seat and looked through the windshield at a beat up old Bronco. It was one of the most beautiful sights I'd ever seen.

"You were right," she said. "It wasn't stolen. It was just driven away."

We were only two hundred yards away from the rim, but in a small depression.

"If I had walked this way, I would have avoided spraining my ankle and all the other stuff that happened."

"You can't change fate, Hubie. And you probably wouldn't want to even if you could. If you hadn't chipped your tooth, you wouldn't have seen Sharice until your next regular check-up, and by then she might have met someone else."

"I guess you're right."

"So this is what you thought we would find. This was your hunch."

"It was my hunch, but I wasn't sure we would find it. There's a lot of open territory up here. We could've missed it."

"I don't think so," she said.

She shut off the truck and walked to the Bronco. It looked unchanged. The keys were in it. I opened the door.

"Wait," she said. "Don't touch anything. There could be clues in there."

"What kind of clues?"

"Fingerprints, a thread from a garment, a crumb of food, anything."

"Anything is right. It's over thirty years old. There are probably enough threads in there to weave a blanket and enough food crumbs to feed a rugby team. And how would we find and collect them? We're not CIS professionals."

"That's CSI. But you're right, we need real CSI guys to do this. So we'll have to go back to Albuquerque and report it so they can bring a team out here."

"The police are not going to waste time and money sending a CSI team out to the middle of nowhere to investigate . . . what, illegal parking? There's no crime here."

"There was a murder, Hubert."

"Maybe. But the police are not going to buy that. There's no body."

"There is a body. We just don't know where it is."

"And have no way to find out where it is."

It was sad to see her deflate. "I guess you're right. Even if you tell them there was a body back there, they won't treat it as a murder." She perked up. "We need to find the body."

"How?"

"I don't know, but maybe we can figure it out."

She agreed to let me drive the Bronco back to Albuquerque but insisted I place Kleenex tissues between my hands and the steering wheel.

The battery was dead. Susannah used jumper cables from the truck. I heard the familiar rurrer-rurrer-rurrer of the starter motor.

# 46

We stayed on paved roads the next morning until we hit the dirt one that runs to La Reina.

I tried to convince Susannah to delay the return trip a day or two. My shop had recently been closed so often that people probably thought I was out of business.

She said there isn't much to choose from between a store that is out of business and one that just doesn't have any customers.

We pulled up in front of El Erupto del Rey just past noon and went in for lunch. Ernesto was not on duty but Baltazar *de los ojos* was. I ordered the same thing I'd had the first time, green chile stew.

Susannah's order was partially in Spanish and bizarre. It took me a minute to figure out why she ordered as she did.

In keeping with her professed desire to learn some Spanish, she asked me what *el erupto del rey* means.

"'The King's belch' I answered, and she laughed.

After lunch we drove the short distance to the home of *la curandera* because I didn't want to go uphill using crutches.

La Viuda de Cheche Zaragosa Medrano greeted us at the door and told me again in Spanish that Susannah was not welcome because she was a *bruja*. I explained how that misunderstanding arose. I'm not sure she completely understood the explanation, but she allowed us both to enter.

I asked her to tell me about Carlos Campos Castillo.

Being a person of honor, she asked why I wanted to know.

"*Porque creo que está muerto.*"

She crossed herself. Then she told me about Carlos Campos Castillo. I also asked her a few questions about The Hunting Guide.

Susannah and I sat in the truck afterwards.

"I really do need to learn Spanish. Do you know how hard it is for someone like me to sit there knowing you're getting valuable information that might solve a murder and not be able to understand a word of it?"

Given her personality, I did have an idea of how antsy she must have been, but I didn't tell her that.

"And why did you say *está muerto*?" she asked. "Shouldn't it be *es muerto*?"

"I can see why you would think so. *Es* is normally used for a permanent condition whereas *está* is used for temporary situations."

"Death is about as permanent as it gets, Hubie, so it should be *es muerto*."

She had a point. When you learn a language growing up, the grammar comes naturally. You don't need rules. You just know what word to use. So how could I explain it? "*Está* is also used when a change has taken place. I would say *Susannah es feliz* because you are happy by nature. But if you were not normally happy, but something made you temporarily happy, I would say *Susannah está feliz.*"

"Let me see if I've got it," she said. "Since death is a change, you say *está muerto.* So I assume you say *es viva* for someone who is alive because they haven't yet changed to dead."

Oops. "No, it's *está viva.*"

She stared at me with furrowed brow. "That makes no sense."

"Okay," I said, "forget *ser* and *estar.* That's a complicated lesson for later. What you need to know first is that the Spanish word for 'ice' is *hielo,* not *ojos.*"

"You gave me the wrong word when I asked you for the Spanish word for 'ice'? I thought you spoke it like a native."

"It wasn't my speaking that was the problem. It was my listening. I thought you asked for the Spanish word for 'eyes', so I told you *ojos.*"

"Well, 'eyes' and 'ice' do sound alike, so I guess that's understandable. No harm done except . . . Oh my God. That's why she thought I was a witch. I ordered my Pepsi with eyes. Baltazar did give me a funny look, but I figured it was because my pronunciation was bad. He must think I'm an idiot."

"Or a witch," I said.

"So what did she tell you about The Dead Guy?"

I took a deep breath. "She said he was a gentle young boy who was always quiet and polite. He loved God. He loved the church. He loved learning the catechism and making his first confession. She always imagined he would be a priest. But after he reached puberty, he became increasingly obsessed with sin. He went to confession so often that the old priest started limiting the days and hours he would take confessions because he didn't have enough time to attend to his other duties. He eventually joined the Penitentes."

"The old priest joined the Penitentes?"

"No, Carlos did. It was one of those village secrets everyone knew and no one talked about. After his parents died, he lived alone in their house. He became increasingly reclusive. No one ever saw him except at church. The house began to deteriorate. He didn't have a job, didn't want one. He would have starved but neighbors brought him food. He would thank them and tell them he would pray for them."

"This is a sad story, Hubie. I can picture him alone in a falling down house praying day and night. So what happened next?"

"That's all she told me."

"Shoot. It's like a story without an ending. I hate that."

"I think I know the ending."

Her face sagged. "He's dead, isn't he?"

"I think so. Remember what Whit told me about Carlos leaving town?" I didn't want to call him The Dead Guy now that I feared he actually was. It seemed disrespectful.

"Yeah," she said. "His booby-trapped piece of firewood blew up in The Hunting Guide's face, so he ran away to avoid revenge."

"I think that story is false."

"Why?"

"Two reasons. First, Carlos doesn't sound like the sort of person who would put gun powder in a piece of firewood. He was a gentle soul. Second, when The Hunting Guide reported the incident, he said he had started growing a beard to cover the scar the ember left on his face. But beards don't grow on scar tissue."

"Really?"

"Yep. I learned that from Cactus Truesdell who had a scar on his cheek where he shot out his tooth."

"Oh brother. You still believe that?"

"That may not be how he got the scar, but it's true there was no beard on it. I saw that with my own eyes."

"Or your own ice."

I chuckled at that and said, "Right. So The Hunting Guide lied. The truth is that he's probably the one who booby-trapped the wood. And he grew the beard so that he could say there was a scar under there. He didn't know beards don't grow on scar tissue."

"So it was Carlos who took the wood."

"He had no electricity. He was probably on the verge of freezing to death. He takes a few pieces of wood. Then the wood blows up. What do you imagine he thought?"

"That God was punishing him for taking the wood. And that The Hunting Guide would come after him. But he had no money. Where did he go?"

"I don't know. La Viuda de Zaragosa told me he had three sisters and three brothers, all of whom were quite a bit older than Carlos. He was evidently a late surprise child like me. The siblings had all moved away by the time Carlos took his first confession. Maybe one of them lives in a nearby village. Or maybe Carlos hitchhiked to Albuquerque. Or maybe he was eaten by a bear. After all, the story I'm telling you is ninety percent conjecture."

"Yeah, but it makes sense. Is there any way we can confirm it?"

"Maybe someone could track down his siblings and find out what they know. But we don't have the means to do that."

"The police could do it."

I sighed. "He's been listed as missing for six months, and they haven't looked for him. Why would they do it now?"

"Because he's been murdered."

"We've already been over that. There is no proof he was murdered."

"What about the fact that The Hunting Guide lied to the police?"

"I guess they could confront him with that, but what good would it do? He could just say it turned out to be a superficial wound, and it healed."

"Maybe they could use rubber hoses to make him confess."

I frowned at her and she laughed.

We sat in silence for a while.

"This is frustrating, Hubie. You finally come around to my view that there was a murder and you even know how it happened, but there's no way to prove it."

"Luring someone into participating in a mock crucifixion is not murder."

"It isn't *mock* when someone dies. If it isn't murder, it should at least be negligent homicide or something."

"Either way, the police don't have sufficient reason to act."

"So we just go home and forget it?"

I shrugged.

She started the engine.

"Go to the church," I said.

She laughed. "Why? You want to make another confession?"

"No, I want to ask Father Jerome how to contact the woman who gave him that pot. I'd like to get another one by her if she will let me have it on consignment. She does good work. I might make a few bucks retailing one of her pots."

"Too bad you can't go back to that cliff dwelling and find a pot for free."

"I tried that before I discovered the body was missing, remember?" I shook my head in disbelief. "In all my years of digging, I've never seen a place with absolutely nothing buried. Two trips there and all I got was one measly shard."

"I guess they were a tidy tribe, Hubie."

She drove to the church.

I was deep in thought. Not about confession or the woman who made the pot, but about why the soil in the cliff dwelling contained almost no record of human habitation and why it was not compacted. Why it was so easy to push the rebar in when I searched the entire area with no results.

"Are you going in?" she finally asked.

"What? Oh, yeah. And after I find out about the potter, I'm going to ask Father Jerome where The Hunting Guide lives. I want to pay him a visit."

The potter was surprised and happy that I wanted one of her pots and didn't hesitate to give it to me on consignment.

The Hunting Guide's house was set back off the road facing a trail against a hill. Susannah stopped about fifty yards from the house, and I used the crutches to circle around to the door.

"I'll be right back," I said.

I wasn't.

# 47

He was even meaner looking than I remembered. And there were no bald spots in his beard.

"Yeah?" he said, blocking his front door.

"Father Jerome told me you lived here," I said, trying to put things on a friendly footing by mentioning the local priest. "I was hoping to hire you as a guide."

He looked me up and down with disdain. "You don't look much like a hunter."

"I've never been hunting. That's why I need a guide. I don't know how to go about it."

"Then why do you want to do it?"

"I like the taste of elk."

He stood there staring at me as if wondering whether he wanted to hire himself out to this tenderfoot at his door. It took him a long time to decide.

He finally stepped back from the door and said, "Come in."

He closed the door and said, "Wait here."

He went into another room and came back with a gun. It was then I realized I was in deep elk excrement. Because even a greenhorn like me knows you don't hunt elk with a pistol.

"This way," he said, motioning me into the room where he'd gone to get the gun. There were a lot of other ones in there, all rifles. There were also shelves of artifacts.

Try as I might, I couldn't think of a reason why he would point a pistol at me if he didn't intend to kill me. He was bigger and stronger than me by far and didn't need a pistol to make me do whatever he wanted me to do.

In fact, he didn't even need a pistol to kill me. I was certain he could do it with his bare hands. But a pistol would be easier.

The reason I was thinking about this was because if there was any possibility that his intent was to teach me how to shoot a pistol or scare me or do something other than kill me, I didn't want to risk running and have him shoot me because I was running just as Billy the Kid shot Deputy James Bell because he was running. I know that's not the sharpest reasoning I've ever done, but it's what I was thinking.

I thought of Billy the Kid's letter to Lew Wallace in which he said, "I would not like to be killed like a dog unarmed."

If I decide, I thought to myself, that he's definitely going to kill me, I don't want to just stand here and be executed. I want to dash for the door or leap through a window.

What I just told you might give you the impression I was a cool customer, calculating his intent and my options while staring down the barrel of a .45 or a .32 or a six-and-a-half. I don't know one gun from another. I would say this one was definitely not a Saturday night special. This was a whole week's worth of gun.

So let me correct any misimpression that I was coolly reasoning. Because I wasn't. I was reasoning, but not calmly. It was amazing I could think at all since my heart had stopped beating. I know your heart is supposed to race in the face of danger, and that's what normally happens to me when I climb higher than the third rung on a ladder. But in this case, my heart just stopped beating. Which didn't matter. Because if it had pumped a bunch of blood to my lungs, the blood couldn't have taken in any oxygen because I also wasn't breathing. All my organs seemed to have shut down. There was an eerie silence, a slowing down of time. It was like I was already dead.

Of course he didn't kill me. If he had, I wouldn't be telling you about that bazooka in his hand and the bizarre physiological effects it had on me.

Emerson said, "War educates the senses, calls into action the will . . ."

It's a good thing I'm not a soldier. Having a gun pointed at me neither educated my senses nor called me to action. It petrified me.

"Out that way," he said, motioning again with the gun towards a door at the back of the room. Since he was waving with his cannon/pointer for me to go first, I decided as soon as I exited the door, I would turn left and run for it.

Unfortunately, I couldn't do that because I was unconscious when I passed through that door. Or maybe it was a different door. All I know is the door was the last thing I saw before a sudden explosion of pain.

I woke up as he was dragging me along a path that was all too familiar. I was hogged tied, and I thought my lips and nose were about to be ripped off by the rough basalt gravel on the path to the cliff dwelling.

I spat the dirt out of my mouth when we got to the dwelling and said, "Why are you doing this?"

His lips were as dark as his beard. "I saw you down here digging. I was standing on the ledge watching you."

So that was why the sand and gravel fell on me. "You drove my Bronco away."

"You left it running, *puto*. Because of you, I had to dig up Carlos. I had to worry about the cops finding out he was dead. And about them finding out about the stuff I took from here. So now I won't have to worry, because you'll be dead. Neat, huh? You're the only outsider who knows about this place. And now you'll be buried in it."

A sinister smile crept across his face. "Buried. Yeah. I like the sound of that. Why waste a slug on a shrimp like you. I'll just throw you in the hole and shovel dirt on your sorry ass."

The good news was my heart was now working, and it was racing like it should have been in light of what it had just heard.

"You won't get away with it," I said, proving that when people are in tight spots, they do indeed say stupid things just like in the movies. "I'm not the only outsider who knows about this place."

He stopped to think for just a second. "Yeah? Who else knows?"

"A friend of mine."

"What's his name."

"I'm not going to tell you. But if you let me go, I promise not to tell the police what happened here."

He laughed. "You won't be telling anyone anything. And before I'm through with you, I'll have the name of that friend."

He turned the gun so that he was holding it by the barrel with the grip sticking out like a hammer.

I decided my best chance—as rotten as it was—was to see if I could somehow roll myself off the ledge. Even if I didn't survive the fall, it was better than being beaten and buried alive.

But he had me tied too tight. He knelt down next to me and raised the pistol butt.

I closed my eyes.

A shot rang out, and he screamed in pain.

*Yes!* I said to myself. *The stupid bastard has accidentally shot himself because he was holding the gun backwards.*

He stood up and turned around. The gun was on the ground next to me where he had dropped it. I tried to nudge it over the cliff using my head since my arms were tied. I was not quite close enough to move it.

I looked up at him. Blood was flowing from his right arm, but not fast enough to suit me. I wanted a waterfall of it. I wanted him unconscious. Actually, I wanted him dead.

He reached down for the gun with his left hand, and a second shot rang out just as he touched the pistol.

*Yes! He's shot himself again.* Then I thought, *How can a hunting guide be so incompetent with a gun?*

Then I heard a voice from above. An angelic voice. It was not telling me I had miraculously been spared. It wasn't even speaking to me. It was coming from the ledge above and was speaking instead to Alonso Castillo Maldonado and saying, "You move a muscle and I'll blow your balls off."

That Susannah is a hell of a shot with a coyote rifle.

# 48

"It was like one of Annie Oakley's stunts in Buffalo Bill's Wild West show," I said to Martin. "First she shot his right arm. Then when he tried to pick up the gun with his left hand, she shot that arm too."

"Two for two," he said, tipping his Tecate can in her direction. "That's good shooting."

"Yeah," I said. "And that's why he took what she said so seriously and stood there as immobile as a marble statue."

"What did she say?"

"She said, 'You move a muscle and I'll blow your balls off'."

Martin gave that little involuntary wince men experience when something of that nature is mentioned.

I turned to Susannah. "I never knew you were such a crack shot."

"It was no big deal, Hubie. I was only thirty feet away. Matt, Mark and I practice with Coors beer cans at a hundred yards."

"You can hit a beer can at a hundred yards?"

"Matt and Mark can hit the can. I hit the little picture of the waterfall on the label of the can."

"How did you know they'd be down in that cliff dwelling," asked Martin.

"I saw The Hunting . . . No, I don't think I'll call him The Hunting Guide any longer. I think I'll call him *El Raton*. I need to practice my Spanish. I saw his jeep leave by the trail in front of his house with what I thought was someone lying down on the back seat. I figured it was Hubie, so I followed him, staying way back so as not to be spotted. When he turned east off the road, I guessed he was headed to the cliff dwelling. I'd been there twice, so I took off across country in the general direction and got there in the nick of time. I saw the jeep and just hoped I wasn't too late. I grabbed the coyote rifle and ran to the edge just as *El Raton* was lifting his arm to club Hubie with his gun butt."

Martin looked at my face then back at her. "Too bad you didn't get there before he did it."

"She did," I said. "This happened when he dragged me over a basalt trail."

"Ouch."

"What I don't understand," Susannah said, "is why you went to his house to begin with."

"Because I'm an idiot."

They looked at each other and nodded.

"Thanks. What happened was I finally thought about the obvious. The second time I was there, I had gone over the entire surface of that cliff dwelling with a rebar, inserting it every six inches. It slid in easily. The soil was not compacted. But I never hit a single artifact. There was one shard the first time, but none on the second visit. No animal skin, no arrowheads, no flint, no worked stone, no broken metates, nothing, zip, *nada*. In over twenty years of digging, I've never encountered a site so totally picked clean."

"But how did you know it was *El Raton*?"

"I didn't. I suspected him because, being a guide, he's always exploring out in the wilds so he would know about it. More importantly, he had a connection with the guy I thought had been buried down there. And finally because he looked like a dangerous felon."

"I was with you until that last one," Susannah said. "You steal pots, and no one would say you look like a dangerous felon."

Then she took another look at me and said, "Well, they might say that the way you look now."

"So," I continued, "I figured I would tip the BLM about him. Maybe they would arrest him for breaking ARPA and NAGPRA, and in the course of their investigation, they might find out something about Carlos."

"So why didn't you just tip the BLM and let them handle it?" Susannah asked.

"Because as I kept telling you, there was no evidence of any crime. I was only guessing that *El Raton* had stolen artifacts from that site, and a judge won't issue a search warrant based on a guess."

"So you wanted to see for yourself."

"I figured I'd visit on the ruse of needing a guide. If I saw any artifacts, I could report it to the BLM and maybe a judge would issue a search warrant since they would have an eyewitness. I figured I'd be there five minutes, tops. I never even considered that it might be risky."

Susannah said, "Even though *El Raton* is in jail, we still don't know for certain that he enticed Carlos into being crucified or even if Carlos was really the dead guy. If they can't prove anything about Carlos, maybe *El Raton* will get off."

I shook my head. "No way, they have an airtight case for attempted murder—mine."

I turned to Susannah and said for about the hundredth time, "You saved my life."

"Yeah. Now I'm responsible for you. So I can't let you endanger yourself by driving an old Crown Vic. I know how to handle the oversteer. You don't. On top of that, you have your Bronco back."

"So you're not going to honor our wager?"

"I am not."

"Thanks."

"I'm not even going to ask," said Martin, and he signaled Angie for a second round for the three of us.

# 49

"Ay Oo You Seh I mu no lie you?"

Sharice laughed and said, "I say you must not like me because first you wear a cast which limits us to kissing and now you've injured your lips, so we can't do even that."

Dr. Batres returned to remove the clip. "You're lucky to have me as your dentist. Repairing the same tooth twice is difficult."

"No as difficuh as bwaken it twice," I replied.

He laughed and departed.

Sharice said she was due a coffee break, so we went to the staff room which had one of those high-tech coffee makers where you insert a small sealed plastic container, and the machine sucks out whatever is in there and turns it into coffee. The advantage of those machines is you can select all sorts of coffee. But what's inside those little plastic things?

Sharice selected Italian Espresso and laughed when I selected Jamaican Surprise.

She asked me to tell her how I was injured. When I reached the point in the narrative where I discovered that Father Jerome was a Dominican, she smiled and asked, "Do you know what Dominicans are called in Canada?"

"Dominicans, eh?"

"No, silly. They're called the 'Black Friars'."

"Because of their *cappa nera*."

"Right. And the Carmelites are called the "White Friars" because of the white cloak which covers their habit."

After I finished my story, she handed me the little baggie with the travel-size toothpaste, tiny spool of floss and two toothbrushes, one white and one black.

"Let me guess," I said. "I get two toothbrushes because it's my second visit in a month, and I get plain black and white because I complained about the bright orange one you tried to pawn off on me the last time."

"Not even close."

"Hmm. One toothbrush is from the Dominicans and one is from the Carmelites."

She shook her head.

"Okay," I said, "I give up."

"The white one is yours. The black one is mine. You can keep it at your place just in case."

"So after my lips heal and my cast comes off—"

"Maybe. But there's something I'll have to tell you first."

# 50

When I opened for business that afternoon, I sold two pots. Maybe that pent up demand thing does sometimes work.

I was behind the counter watching a tall man dressed in blue jeans and a pearl-buttoned western shirt examine the pot I'd made based on the shard.

He finally turned my way. "Is this genuine?"

"Absolutely. I know that because I made it."

"Hmm. I thought it was old."

"I made it to look old."

"It's a copy of an ancient pot?"

I nodded.

"I like the design," he said. "I've never seen one like it."

I retrieved the shard from my workshop and handed it to him. "This is from an ancient pot. I'm certain it's pre-Columbian."

"So this was your pattern."

"And my inspiration."

"Where did the shard come from?"

"Here in New Mexico."

He smiled. "And that's as specific as you're going to get."

I nodded again.

"This isn't old, but it is one of a kind," he said, mostly to himself. "How much is it?"

I had been trying to decide that a while back when I realized the pot I made and the one Father Jerome brought me were not from the same tribe. That took my thoughts down another path, and I had never come back to the matter of price. I normally price my copies at ten percent of what the original is worth. If I had the entire pot of which the shard was a piece, I would ask fifty thousand for it.

"Five thousand," I said.

"That sounds high for a copy."

"Like you said, it's unique."

"So it is." He thought for a moment. "Throw in the shard, and I'll take it."

Now it was my turn to think. It didn't take me long to decide.

"I can't do that." I said.

"Why not?"

"I have other plans for it."

"You want it as a model for further copies?"

"No."

"I'll give you three thousand for the pot."

"You think the shard is worth two thousand?"

"Not by itself. But it makes the pot more interesting because it's the genuine piece from which the pot was designed. It would be worth five thousand to me to be able to display them together."

"Sorry, but I can't sell the shard. And I can't take three thousand for the pot."

"Thirty five hundred cash. Final offer."

"Sold."

As I was boxing up the pot, its new owner asked what happened to my face.

"I was dragged down a rough trail to the spot where that shard was found."

He shook his head in wonderment. "Surely there must have been an easier way to get there."

I've been known, after making a sale, to close the shop for the rest of the day in celebration. And also because what are the odds of my making two sales in one day? But I stayed open and did just that.

A tourist visiting with her college-aged daughter bought the pot crafted by the woman in La Reina. I had it priced at twenty-five hundred and she bargained me down to two thousand. I was easy because I empathized with her as a fellow tuition-payer and because I already had thirty five hundred in the till.

"Do you mind if I inquire about your injuries?" she asked as I was running her credit card.

I pointed to my face. "Let this be a warning to you. Always wear sunscreen."

The mother and daughter glanced at each other.

Whit came in just before closing time.

"The sheriff up there said you was dragged to where they arrested Maldonado, but he didn't mention you was dragged on your face."

"I know you didn't come here to comment on my injuries."

"No, I came to bring you up to date like you requested. They reached a deal with Maldonado. He gets total immunity for the dead guy you dug up in return for telling them where the body is."

"Total immunity? What if it turns out he killed the guy?"

"They'd never make that stick. The dead guy was one of those nuts who beat themselves with whips and even volunteer to haul a cross and be tied on it. Sometimes they even get their hands nailed to it. Someone dies under those circumstances, you can't really say they were murdered. They're all just nutcases."

I thought about Carlos. "Maybe most of them are nuts, but some could be saints. Martin says that before you criticize a man, you should walk a mile in his moccasins."

"That's good advice, Hubert."

I was surprised by his positive reaction. "It is?"

"Sure, that way if he don't like your criticism, there ain't much he can do about it because you're a mile away from him and he's barefooted. You want to hear the rest of the deal?"

"I guess."

"He also gets immunity from the pot digging if he returns all the stuff he still has and gives them a list of everyone he sold stuff to. I hope you keep a list of your customers, Hubert, in case you ever need to bargain your way out of your pot thieving."

"I would never betray my customers. So he walks on the cru-cifixion death and the ARPA and NAGPRA charges. What about trying to kill me?"

"They don't think they can stick him with that either."

"What!"

"The law defines attempted murder as taking an action designed to kill, like stabbing you or shooting at you. He didn't do anything that could have killed you."

"That's only because Susannah showed up before he got the chance."

"Don't matter. He took no potentially lethal action against you."

I was flabbergasted. "He told me he was going to kill me."

"Your word against his."

"He tied me up and dragged me down to that cliff dwelling."

"Right, and that's where they got him—kidnapping. Actually, it's aggravated kidnapping since he did you bodily harm. That carries a longer sentence, so it's fortunate that he dragged you."

"Lucky me. How long is the sentence?"

"He bargained for twenty years, but he'll likely serve about twelve if he don't get in trouble in prison or get killed there."

"Great. So in twelve years a guy who tried to kill me will be back on the street and hardened by a dozen years of prison."

"I wouldn't worry about it. I doubt he'll want a return trip. And I'll make sure the APD keeps you safe. The bad news is that they took all the old pots in his house into custody up there, so I didn't have a chance to grab one for you to sell for us. I don't suppose you found one up there?"

"He had picked the site so clean, the only thing left was a shard."

"That's just a piece of one, right?"

"Right, but I sold it for a thousand dollars." I figured five hundred would satisfy him.

He let out a long whistle. "A thousand bucks for a broken piece. No wonder you like being a pot thief."

I gave him the five hundred.

"It ain't the most we ever made," he said, "but it ain't bad for a few phone calls. Nice doing business with you."

# 51

Susannah and I made our final trip to La Reina a couple of weeks later to attend a memorial mass for Carlos Campos Castillo.

After the service, everyone gather at El Erupto del Rey for lunch. Susannah spent several minutes talking to Baltazar *de los ojos* then joined me at our table.

Father Jerome was making the rounds of the tables and booths. When he stopped at ours, he joked that we should be made honorary villagers. La Viuda de Zaragosa came over and thanked me for making it possible for one of their own to be brought home and buried in the churchyard. I thought of my conversation with Consuela.

"I think I'll come back next month on *El Día de los Muertos* to visit Carlos," I said to Susannah.

"What would you bring him?"

"I guess *pan de muerto* and *cempasúchil.*"

"I think I know what *pan de muerto* is, but what is *cempasúchil?*"

"Marigolds."

"I'll come with you."

"You just want to see Baltazar."

"Why not? He seems nice, Hubie. He's my age, handsome, and single. And Sirena lives here, so we could double date."

"Yeah, and I could keep the cast on in case Hugo decides to go a few more rounds with me."

I asked her to stop by the cliff dwelling on the way back.

"The cliff dwelling is not on the way back. It's not on the way to anything."

"It's on the way to trouble. But I want to go there anyway."

"What the heck," she said. "At least I know how to find it."

I looked at the scary mound of boulders at the top of the switchback and told Susannah I wanted to tie a rope to the bottom one. Since I was still in the cast, she volunteered to do it.

After the rope was in place, Susannah activated the winch. When the bottom boulder began to move, the pile above it rumbled down the slope and knocked off part of the cliffside, destroying a section of the path.

"Okay," she said, "now that I've helped you do that, you want to tell me *why* we did that."

"I want the site to be left alone."

I walked over to the ledge above the site, close to where Susannah had been standing when she shot *El Raton*. Not as close to the edge as she had been, but close enough to toss the shard down to where it had come from.

"What is this, some sort of weird cleansing ceremony where you give up pot digging?"

"No, the ancient potters want me to find their work."

"You really believe that? I always figured that was just a rationalization you liked."

"I do believe it. The Indians who sell their stuff in Old Town are proud of it, as they should be. But just because they sell their arts and crafts doesn't mean they sell their culture. I can take a pot from an ancient site and leave the site undisturbed. It's a perfect analogy."

"If you say so."

"I've been worrying about being associated with the people who destroy sites in the process of looting them, but I've resolved my concerns about that."

"If you hadn't gone down there, Carlos would still be in an unknown and unmarked grave. So some good did come from your pot digging."

"I've been thinking how weird it is that there's a book about Billy the Kid written by Pat Garrett, the man who shot him down in cold blood."

"This has something to do with Carlos?"

"It does. Evidently there were a lot of hucksters after Billy's death claiming they had his pinky finger, his skull or some other part of him. They would travel around and charge people to see those things."

"I'm glad we don't have those sorts of shameless exhibitions these days."

"Yeah. We have reality television instead. Anyway, at the end of the book, Garrett goes to great lengths to say that all those claims are false, that Billy was given a proper burial and his grave had not been disturbed. He also rails against the reporters and editorialists who criticized him in various newspapers for shooting Billy in cold blood. And the rest of the book is about how Billy had many sterling qualities."

"Sounds like Garrett had a load of guilt."

"That's what I thought." I was looking over the deep canyon

of the Rio Doloroso at the Jemez Mountains in the blue distance. There is something spiritual about the long vistas in New Mexico. "Billy was given a proper burial. Carlos was hidden away in an unmarked grave. Frank Aguirre's ashes were dumped into an irrigation ditch." I looked at her. "You think it makes any difference?"

She started to answer then suddenly looked over my shoulder and said, "I do not believe this!"

I turned to see Wiley trotting towards me, my hat hanging from his mouth. He stopped about twenty feet from me and dropped it. Then he stared at me for a few seconds and trotted away. I remembered Julie the vet telling me that dogs have a nesting instinct and like to take soft personal items from their owners as a show of affection. Maybe he *had* seen me as a helper. Maybe he *did* dig that water for us. Maybe that *was* a smile on his face. Probably not, but I liked the idea.

I turned back around.

"You're crying," she said.

"Tears of joy," I said. "Let's go home."

# Acknowledgments

Many of you know that the working title of this sixth book in the series was *The Pot Thief Who Studied Lew Wallace.* I changed it to *The Pot Thief Who Studied Billy the Kid* for reasons that should be evident in the story.

As always, I want to thank my wife Lai without whom none of my work would ever be completed.

I am also grateful to my daughter Claire and to Linda Aycock and Ofélia Nikolova for their editing support.

Special thanks to Mike Norman, author of the Sam Kincaid and J. D. Books mysteries, two excellent series. By some quirk of fate, Mike was a professor in the criminal justice program at Weber State University in Utah, and I was his dean. Mike's J. D. Books is a Park Ranger, and Mike is fond of saying that his protagonist would like to put mine in jail.

Mike has allowed me to piggyback on his research. Which

makes sense because he was an excellent teacher and researcher, and his decision to become a writer was a loss to the academic world.

I was not an excellent researcher. I like to think that my move from academia to mystery writing improved both areas.

Finally, I want to thank the legions of Hubie fans. The royalty checks are nice, but your letters and emails are the best reward for my writing.

# About the Author

J. Michael Orenduff grew up in a house so close to the Rio Grande that he could Frisbee a tortilla into Mexico from his backyard. While studying for an MA at the University of New Mexico, he worked during the summer as a volunteer teacher at one of the nearby pueblos. After receiving a PhD from Tulane University, he became a professor. He went on to serve as president of New Mexico State University.

Orenduff took early retirement from higher education to write his award-winning Pot Thief murder mysteries, which combine archaeology and philosophy with humor and mystery. Among the author's many accolades are the Lefty Award for best humorous mystery, the Epic Award for best mystery or suspense ebook, and the New Mexico Book Award for best mystery or suspense fiction. His books have been described by the *Baltimore Sun* as "funny at a very high intellectual level" and "deliciously delightful," and by the *El Paso Times* as "the perfect fusion of murder, mayhem and margaritas."

# THE POT THIEF MYSTERIES

FROM OPEN ROAD MEDIA

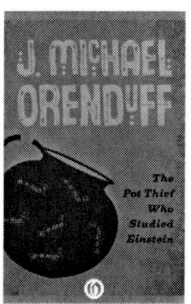

Available wherever ebooks are sold

OPEN ROAD
INTEGRATED MEDIA

OPEN ROAD

INTEGRATED MEDIA

**Open Road Integrated Media** is a digital publisher and multimedia content company. Open Road creates connections between authors and their audiences by marketing its ebooks through a new proprietary online platform, which uses premium video content and social media.

## Videos, Archival Documents, and New Releases

Sign up for the Open Road Media newsletter and get news delivered straight to your inbox.

Sign up now at
www.openroadmedia.com/newsletters

FIND OUT MORE AT
WWW.OPENROADMEDIA.COM

FOLLOW US:
@openroadmedia and
Facebook.com/OpenRoadMedia

CPSIA information can be obtained at www.ICGtesting.com
Printed in the USA
LVOW10s1532150415

434708LV00001B/125/P

9 781480 458628